DRIVI

CW01636919

Previously published under the Title The Voice
ISBN 978-1-910236-66-6 Paperback
978-1-910236-67-3 Kindle

Driven to murder

First paperback edition printed in 2021 in the United Kingdom

A catalogue record for this book is available from the British Library

ISBN
Paperback 978-1-915742-07-0
Kindle 978-1-915742-06-3

Published by The Creative Peak(TCP)

Book Design: T M Goble
Cover Image: Copyright Shutterstock

T M Goble's Website

www.tmgoble.com

Action Thrillers
Detective Murder Mysteries
Standalone Murder Mysteries
Historical Fiction
Contemporary Fiction
History of Peak District Literature
Seasonal Recipes
I occasionally send newsletters with details on new releases, special offers and other bits of news relating to my books.

01

Evelyn pulled her coat tight as she stepped from the office building into the midday gloom of November. The road offered a short walk for lunchtime fruit from the convenience store at the nearby garage. The grey mist enveloped the offices and extended over the dull green fields.

Had she achieved her aim? Her stomach twisted with excitement, as perhaps she had. Confidence wrestled through her body. The first steps to her new life. A smile creased her lips at her initial success.

The decision would come this afternoon. While she might win, the future held trepidation. Could she cope with the closeness of the other three? Would they rely on her? Office life could become difficult, but the three months had passed without a major incident, so her confidence remained strong.

The open countryside gave her a sense of freedom, but the heavy drone of the distant lorries on the motorway refocused her thoughts on her job. Pursing her lips, the boss of the company had employed her. The lust in his eyes had dominated the interview. Grateful for his focus on her body, he had given only a quick check of the documents that she had supplied as proof of her qualifications.

Would he make a pass at her? She smiled. He would, especially if she won the competition. Would she concede? Probably because it would be to her benefit and she could reap fine rewards.

Turning past the trees towards the busy roundabout, she grimaced at the noise and pulled up the hood on her anorak as she crossed the forecourt of the petrol station to the store. Turning her nose up at the smell of petrol, the store came as a relief from the lorry drone and polluted atmosphere.

Expecting to win the imminent decision, a bar of chocolate for each would express team solidarity. Moving to the back of the store, she picked an orange and a Golden Delicious apple for lunch. Browsing the laden shelves in the compact store, she selected a carton of passata for her evening meal and stopped at the chocolate display. With her back towards the security camera, she slipped three bars of chocolate into her pocket.

Closing her eyes momentarily, she screwed up her face on approaching the counter to contend with the over-the-top owner of the store. She couldn't fault his enthusiasm, but his ebullience overwhelmed her. An overweight man with little left of his hair, the smile never left his face.

'Hello, darling. Better weather today. The sunshine is peeking through the fog, but the breeze is chilled.'

Evelyn handed him the apple, orange and passata. She could only manage the faintest of smiles from within the anorak hood, which she had not pushed back on entering the store. 'Three items that's £2.38. Golden delicious, my favourite. We share similar tastes.' The brief smile returned. She rarely spoke to him, but he never took offence. 'And, the passata. My favourite is a good chilli. Is that what you are making for your hubby tonight?'

The sexist comment sent a shiver through her body, but he had an unnatural knack of guessing what she would have for her supper when she had picked one item. She didn't like people second guessing her actions.

Leaving the store without a smile, she pulled her silk scarf across her face to keep out the fumes. Her life outside of work needed more thought, as she had become a recluse. Focusing on the predictable nine to five routine, her social life had been put on hold. Control was needed. On occasions she had descended into despicable behaviour, but at twenty-five years old she should be able to enjoy life and not break social niceties.

02

Simon focused on Evelyn's tight black trousers as she strolled along the pavement after her usual lunchtime visit to the garage shop. Slowing his run, he wanted to take full advantage of her shapely backside before overtaking her. He'd hankered after her tall frame and slender body since she'd joined the company. Her lack of smiling and her dismissive attitude annoyed him, but he would persist.

The steady pounding of his trainers on the tarmac echoed as he closed on her. He had one last long look but needed to appear casual. 'Hi, Evelyn.' Sprinting past, he couldn't resist glancing over his shoulder at the front view of her figure, although he could see little in the padded jacket. She gave a small flick of her hand, but his presence raised no smile.

Rubbing his face at the unexpected distraction of her, he settled into his stride as the stress of the impending decision returned. The tension had pushed up his blood pressure during the morning. The forced jollity of Dan and Sadie had annoyed him, so he hoped a run would calm him, but tension still gripped his stomach.

Despite concentrating on his jogging, the worry of his job wouldn't leave him. Would he be successful? Adrenaline coursed through his veins and he quickened his pace. The cool air glided across his skin. Sweating and puffing, he bounded around the corner of an office block as he tried to suppress the negative thoughts whirling in his mind. He must stop fantasising about Evelyn, as it disrupted his carefully planned work schedule.

His worry had intensified over the last few weeks and had reached its peak before lunch. Unable to face eating and the continual chatter of Dan and Sadie, he had opted to leave the office. In the distance, the turning came to leave the industrial park, cross the main road and enjoy a countryside lane. The quiet would offer release from the busy roads close to the industrial park. The country lane had plantations of trees with tracks to drift or sprint along. Today it would be drifting.

While the distant drone of the traffic continued, the sweet smell of the woods was a pleasure. After sprinting for twenty yards, he reined back to a jog. The wood had not provided the sanctum of calmness he wanted as the pressures of the job scattered his mind.

Nervous and meticulously obsessed since a young boy about time, he gave a flick of his watch to see the date. Three months to the day he'd joined the start-up technology business, TechMatt as team leader. The simple anniversary should have been a celebration, but he battled to stay calm and revel in the experience. The four had worked in a team, although his job of coordinating their efforts had presented an uphill battle.

Today's crucial decision would dictate the next few months. Whichever proposal was chosen, the other three would be committed to work on it. Dan and Sadie had disappointed him. Their skills were weak. Evelyn was a mystery and shared no clue of her work within the broad remit they had been given.

The cold November air bit into his lungs and pinked the exposed skin of his arms and legs. The jog had warmed him, although he agonised about the afternoon and checked his pulse. Far too high for a gentle jog. The public footpath led him through the Manor Hotel grounds. Two Ziani cars gleamed in the sunlight that had broken through the fog at the electric charging point. The smartly suited owners chatted.

He sighed as he drifted past at low speed. Unless he made a success of his career, he would be lucky to pass beyond his Ford Focus. Trying to shrug his negative thoughts aside, he jogged from the hotel grounds to approach the stinking road jammed with lorries. The driver of a stationary lorry waved him across. With the further carriageway clear, he sprinted to the safety of the industrial park and resumed his gentle jog. There would be no explosive bursts because of his high blood pressure.

The dismal flower beds and the left-over roadwork barriers presented a forlorn picture as he approached the ground floor of the new building. The first door led him under the illuminated sign, TechMatt. Pausing for a few cool down stretches, he pushed open the door to the office suite where he worked. The decision that would come this afternoon would make or break his role in the fledgling company. Perhaps the high-pressure start-up had been the wrong move and a Civil Service job in the centre of Sheffield would have been less stressful for him.

Bringing his thoughts back to the reality of the afternoon, he would focus on business after his post-run shower. He grimaced as Sadie shrieked. Dan and her playing table tennis were a nightmare. Whatever had Aaron considered the purpose of the installation? It was not his idea and caused him severe irritation. He came to the office to work and not to play table tennis. Flicking at his watch again, his blood pressure had risen.

03

Aaron strode across the green carpet to his office window. The mist of the grey November afternoon bleached the colour from the office blocks and the car park. Within the greyness, his shiny bright gun-metal grey Ziani car glowed. He admired the sleek lines of his car which he had parked at the end of the row. Ahmed had parked his black Ziani at a strange angle in the next bay.

Desperate for a decision that would bring him profit, his money would run out in three months. Ahmed's money would help keep them afloat in the short term, but he invested in risk and could change his mind if the prospects were poor. Candice exacerbated his problem, as despite many hints, she had not curtailed her excessive social spending, which added to her frequent expensive shopping trips to London, Paris, and Milan.

The giggling and excitement of Sadie and Dan playing table tennis in the outer office percolated through the closed door. Dan guffawed, resulting in a shriek from Sadie. He never knew whether Simon and Evelyn were there, as they offered a silent contribution to the atmosphere in the office. Sadie had an infectious giggle which contrasted with Dan's deep laugh.

Twisting away from the grey landscape with a frown of fierce concentration, his eyes fixed on Candice and Ahmed, who occupied chairs near his desk. The strained silence contrasted with the noisy enthusiasm from Dan and Sadie. His wife's thumbs skated over the screen of her mobile phone. The pink manicured nails caught the light as her fingers flicked. Why did Candice receive and send so many texts?

Ahmed pecked away at his iPad. Their silent absorption increased Aaron's irritation. Closeted in his office for hours, they had read and reread the four proposals from his employees but had made no progress in deciding which one should be selected for future development.

He ran his fingers through his short brown hair. No solution had become obvious. Too much time and money had been poured into this venture for it to fail. The decision-making meeting had drifted because agreement eluded them.

Ahmed had invested money, which currently gave no return. A hard-nosed businessman who had made his fortune in the City of London's financial sector, he wouldn't be happy for his lack of monetary return to continue.

Alarm bells rang in Aaron's mind as he recalled the discussions which had taken place during the day. Ahmed had become irritated as they'd reiterated the same points. Worry mingled with frustration and the knot in his stomach tightened. With growing consternation, he glanced away from Ahmed and focused on his wife.

Candice had dressed in an elaborate pale grey Armani suit coupled with a simple pink blouse and a subtle string of pearls. Her long blonde hair caught the light from the desk lamp. Immaculate make-up stressed the angular cheekbones of her attractive face. The heart-shaped lips, sporting a shocking pink lipstick, pouted as she focused on her phone. He'd fallen for her when they first met. The moment remained fresh in his mind. She'd been with colleagues for an early evening drink on their way home from work. Ahmed had introduced her. By the time she left, they had exchanged phone numbers. From then on, it had been a whirlwind romance, and they'd married six months later.

Their fifth anniversary would come soon, and he would take her somewhere exotic. The thought cheered him as he pictured them lounging by the pool of an exclusive hotel, sipping cocktails and watching the sun set over the ocean.

With a shake of his head, he blocked the thoughts to return to the decision. Had Simon done a good job of gathering the four proposals? Possibly, but as team leader he should be sure of the winner, but he had given no signs of leadership. Perhaps it had been a poor decision to appoint him, but it was too late. Ahmed and Candice must agree on a decision today, so he would be forceful and guide them to a solution.

04

The silence in the office increased Simon's apprehension as he entered after showering. The tension stretching through his body hadn't dissipated. Evelyn, Sadie, and Dan sat at their desks, but wouldn't be working. As team leader should he check? He dismissed the idea as he could not concentrate on work as they waited. The knot in his stomach tightened. Why couldn't Aaron decide? Simon hovered in the doorway, but no one lifted their heads or acknowledged his arrival. The unenthusiastic tapping of the keyboards filled the outer office. They waited the same as him.

Dan would be gaming. Sadie would be on Facebook, as always. Little sound emerged from Evelyn's desk. Her activities remained a mystery. Whenever he walked behind her, she swapped screens to conceal her work. The secretive approach irritated him. What had she to hide?

The dull grey light from the windows matched his mood. The stagnant aroma from the open kitchen in the corner of the office wafted through the space. The residue of Dan's microwave lasagne made his stomach recoil. Frowning, he would not have placed the four desks back-to-back in a Maltese Cross. Aaron, the boss, had chosen the arrangement to help their concentration.

Simon preferred eye contact. Slumping into his chair the team leader role weighed heavy. A bar of Dairy Milk chocolate held the central position on his desk. He hadn't bought it. Dan guessed his reaction. 'Evelyn bought us a present.'

'Thanks.' Sneering at his screen, his voice had been bland, he could have visited her desk and smiled.

Sadie's curled brown hair caught the light as she returned a dirty mug to the kitchen. He studied her lithe figure. Her friendly demeanour and sparkling enthusiasm often made him smile, but the enigmatic Evelyn held a greater attraction for him. Her secretive nature had aroused his interest and he wanted to delve deep into her thoughts, but he would have to surmount her frosty attitude.

Sadie ran her fingers through her hair. Wisps bounced in the light giving hints of a rainbow. Returning to her chair, she swivelled to face him. He'd been caught watching her. He raised his eyebrows and Sadie beamed a smile back. 'They've been in there for hours. When will we have the decision?'

05

The sweat formed on Aaron's forehead. The black clouds of collapsed finances loomed on the horizon. 'We have been in here for hours.' Striding from the window, he dropped into his seat.

Ahmed closed his iPad with a decisive slap. Candice slid her phone into her bag. With a pinched expression, she studied her nails before her eyes drifted to the wall clock, 'I'm bored. We are going in circles. The only proposal worth considering is Simon's.'

He loved his wife but why she wanted to become involved in the business, he had no idea. The company had needed two people to be registered for legal purposes. When he'd told her, he had assumed she would leave the operations to him. But it had piqued her interest. Attending only when it did not clash with a social appointment, her spasmodic involvement was undermined by a lack of technical knowledge.

He attempted to decipher, without success, the expression in her eyes. A sparkle of excitement? Dismissing the ridiculous thought in the middle of a business meeting. Why always support Simon? 'You cannot justify your choice.'

Ahmed's face twitched, 'You keep quarrelling so we cannot find a closure. I'm a money man, and not technical, but Simon's lifestyle proposal is marketable. Dan's connecting the household together is good as I'd love to have more sophistication in controlling my home from the iPad.'

Aaron sniffed. 'Simon's idea is feasible but has significant competition. Similar products are established in the market. Dan's is better but is he up to delivering a ground-breaking idea? Some aspects of his work are vague and simple systems already exist. By the time we reach market we will be behind the curve and the conglomerates will destroy us.' Bowing his head forward, he rubbed a hand across his aching forehead, 'Why can't we agree? The decision is crucial.' He received blank looks from Ahmed and Candice.

'Aaron,' a gentle voice echoed from the computer speaker.

'Yes!' He curled his lip at the interruption to his thoughts.

'Your diary says your meeting has finished and the next entry requires you to be at home to receive a call from an American technology supplier.' He stared with contempt at the computer.

'The meeting has not finished!'

The disembodied voice continued, 'I'm sorry to interrupt you. I can hear the stress in your voice. Please check your Fitbit to make sure you are not straying out of the target zones for your health parameters.'

'Go away, Dess,' snarled Aaron as a flash of irritation lit up his eyes.

'Will do. Let me know if you want me later. Bye for now.'

Aaron slumped into his chair with a frown. His hands gripped the arms. His throat had dried. Tension gripped him. Time to decide. His forehead puckered in thought. He glanced with narrowed eyes at the computer. 'Dess, are you there?'

'Of course, Aaron.'

'Why did you contact me?'

'I expected you to be going home and as the external temperature is only four degrees, do you want me to adjust the climate control on your Ziani?'

He pursed his lips as he contemplated the information he'd been given. 'Give it thirty minutes and check back with me.'

'Yes, Aaron. And it's good to hear your voice is more relaxed.'

'Go away, Dess.'

'Catch you later,' responded the calm, tinny voice.

Candice and Ahmed remained silent. Aaron returned his look to Ahmed and then at his wife. 'You seem surprised.'

Ahmed cleared his throat and pointed a wary finger towards the computer. 'Who or what is Dess?'

'You've never mentioned a Dess before.' Candice sat upright in her chair.

Aaron laughed 'That's Sadie's working prototype of her proposal. She called it Dess because it is the initials of the four in the office.'

Ahmed's brows knitted together. 'Why didn't you tell us about it before?'

'The others didn't have their prototypes in a form to demonstrate so we chose paper proposals to keep it fair.'

'But it's brilliant,' Ahmed pointed towards the computer, 'I can arrange finance to fully develop it.' He thrust a hand through his black hair, nodded, and a slow smile spread across his face.

'I agree with Ahmed. It's exactly what we need.' Candice leaned back in her chair and laughed with delight. 'It's amazing how it detected the stress in your voice. Is that part of Sadie's emotional analysis?'

Aaron leaned forward on his elbows and relaxed. Progress. Ahmed had been impressed; money would flow into the business. Excitement mingled with relief as a smile spread across his face. 'Yes, Simon and Sadie have been talking about how his lifestyle proposal can be linked to the emotional analysis.'

Ahmed studied him with bright, curious eyes. 'Why haven't you asked me to finance more if they can be linked?'

'I expected it would be difficult to get your agreement to one.' Aaron shook his head and gave a small, derisive laugh. 'I had no hope of four. Tell me what you are thinking?'

Ahmed waved a hand towards the computer. 'Dess linked through to your car.'

Aaron dipped his head in acknowledgment and a self-satisfied smile appeared on his face. 'Dan and Sadie get on well. He is fascinated by the car so asked me if he might incorporate it as part of his idea to connect things together.' Aaron leaned back in his chair and gave a small, throaty laugh.

Candice relaxed. With a puzzled expression in her eyes, 'What's so funny?'

'Sadie and Dan linked their ideas together. We've been trying them out. Dess wanted me to drive with care last night as my stress levels were up. It amused me. Not only can the Ziani drive itself, now it's telling me how to drive.' His lips smiled slowly in self-appreciative amusement.

'So will Sadie's Dess link to the other objects that Dan wants to control in his proposal.' Ahmed's voice piqued with curiosity.

'Yes, of course.'

Aaron leaned back in his chair, flexed his hands behind his head. This would be good. The money from Ahmed would underpin a rapid expansion. Relief washed over him, as it had been a long and stressful meeting. 'Simon and Dan's work will integrate well with Sadie's, but Evelyn's needs more work before it's ready.'

'I'm glad we've made progress.' Candice stood. Ahmed studied her for a long moment, his expression unreadable. Then he glanced across at Aaron with an inquiring gleam in his eyes. 'We launch with the triangle of the three and allow Evelyn's to come to market slower but in the background.'

Aaron breathed a long slow breath, allowing the tension to ebb away. 'I'll tell the troops.'

06

Aaron finished his small glass of champagne. He'd announced to the team that the four proposals would be developed. The triangle of three and then on a longer timescale, Evelyn's idea. His mind had whirled since the end of the meeting. Having Ahmed's money on board would be a lifesaver. Excitement, coupled with anticipation, soared through him as he expected to expand the size of the team, which would require a move to larger premises.

Dan and Sadie had been ecstatic when he'd announced the decision. They'd whooped with delight, high fived and ran a lap of honour around the office. The exuberance and excitement became infectious as Aaron had clapped and laughed at their antics. Simon smiled and nodded, but Aaron suspected not with total enthusiasm. Evelyn gave a brief smile, but her normal sombre face had returned. She'd listened to the elated babble of conversation but had remained silent and aloof. Her expression was unreadable. She hadn't drunk her champagne and Sadie had finished it for her.

Before the general chatter of excitement had quietened, Evelyn stood and wandered to her desk. Her response to the decision confused him. Why hadn't she been pleased? What went on inside that intelligent head? She didn't respond to him in the way most women did, as his handsome face and charismatic manner ensured attention. But not from Evelyn. His curiosity increased, so he slipped from his chair and wandered across the office. As he crossed behind her desk, he glanced at her screen, which was black. The window where she had been typing had been closed. Why had she done that? What did she want to hide?

The complicated proposal she had submitted showed her to be an intelligent woman. He'd love to find out what makes her tick. A pang of annoyance shot through him. He could be too busy with the growth of the business to entertain a slow seduction of her. His mind buzzed with impatience. He liked a challenge. A smile spread across his face as he had time before the details were confirmed. Before moving forward with expanding the business, he would wait for the confirmation in writing from Ahmed.

Impulsiveness and self-indulgence combined to force him into action. Evelyn's proposal was good but would need commitment. The other three acted as a team and could deliver the integrated solution so his business would not miss her leaving. He would try. A hint of arrogance glimmered in his eyes. 'Evelyn, can you spare me a few minutes, or do you need to leave?'

'I'm in no rush,' she swivelled to face him, but didn't smile. She rose from her chair and followed him into his office.

Moving to his office chair. 'Come in, Evelyn. Sit down, I wish to talk to you about our decision.' Closing the door with a quiet click, she lowered herself onto the chair in front of his desk. After a smile, which lasted only for a second, she crossed her legs and perched a notebook on her lap. She swept her eyes around the room. 'I can give you as much time as you need.'

Her response confused him as he raked his eyes across her expressionless face. The words and the face didn't match. Her eyes held no clues and her posture was stiff. She stared at the notebook in her lap. She'd rarely been in his office. Perhaps she was overawed sitting alone with her boss. He dismissed the idea at once. When he wanted to speak to his staff, he approached them in the outer office. The others came into his office, but Evelyn never did. Why? Didn't she like him?

His eyes settled on the curve of her lips. Not as shapely as Candice's heart shaped mouth but enticing. Unlike Candice, who wore extensive makeup, Evelyn's face remained natural. Not highly coloured, but healthier than pale.

Candice forever changed her hairstyles, but the long brown hair tied back had never changed in the three months since he'd employed Evelyn. After a lengthy silence, he cleared his throat. 'Your proposal is the best, but it will take longer and more money to develop, but it's included in the plan.'

'Thank you, Aaron. I'm glad you like it.' A smile flickered on her lips and the dark brown eyes focused on him. He wriggled in his chair. An intense woman with hidden depths. Not that he minded. A mixture of interest and challenge moved through him, causing his skin to tingle. With an effort, he refocused.

'Can you do a job for me before we start on your idea?'

'Yes, what do you require?'

'Sadie, Simon and Dan will develop their proposals. Will you lead their integration?'

'With pleasure.' A longer lasting smile stayed.

Encouraged, he grinned. 'Perhaps we can spend time so I can explain my expectations for the integration.'

Her subdued voice dropped to almost a whisper. 'Do you want to do it now?'

'That's the difficulty.' An over dramatic sigh escaped from his lips, 'I must create a plan so that Ahmed can arrange the finance. Then I must find larger premises and recruit more staff.' His dark eyes settled on her. 'It will be difficult to find the time to spend with you.'

'An evening would suit me fine.' Aaron raised his eyebrows. It hadn't been the response he'd expected, but he wouldn't refuse the opportunity of working with Evelyn on her own. Impatience gripped him. He half held his breath as he fought to keep his voice steady. 'Tomorrow?'

'If you prefer to do it away from the office, I would love a chance to have a ride in your car.' Another surprising twist from her.

'I'll include you on the insurance and then you will be able to drive.' Aaron studied her face for several long seconds. 'We'll need to spend time together, so we agree on the way forward.'

A wry smile quirked her mouth. 'I'm sure we will agree on many aspects of the way forward.'

07

Sadie with her mind whirling that she had become the centre of the project closed the frosted glass office door behind her. The chilly air of the entrance foyer hit her and she screwed up her face. It would be colder outside and not a pleasant cycle ride in the dark on the quiet roads that avoided the heavy traffic.

The route, pleasant in daylight, had become scary during the darkness as most of the journey passed through a heavily wooded area. She set Dess on her mobile phone to home travel. The system would continually monitor her and at the first sign of distress in her voice would trigger personal alarms in her pocket and on the bike.

A shudder spread through her body as the euphoria at being selected for her Dess implementation had evaporated. She hadn't expected to be chosen and her weaknesses would be exposed to everyone in the office, including Aaron.

From a rucksack, she retrieved florescent trousers, then balancing on each leg, she dragged them over her jeans. The thick, bright yellow jacket completed her riding clothes. Her reflection in the front door glowed in the harsh light of the foyer. She flicked on the blinking light on her cycle helmet. Ready for the November weather, she stopped at the main door of the office block and waited for Evelyn.

The tension of the day and the celebratory champagne had delayed her. When Aaron made the announcement, she had bubbled with excitement, but reality hit her hard twenty minutes later. Two glasses of champagne normally helped her relax, but not this evening.

Developing Dess had been a struggle and she was concerned that the flaky system might collapse at any minute to reveal critical weaknesses. Long hours of hard work beckoned for her program to become viable commercial software, as it had been hacked together. Asking for help to make the programming more robust would be embarrassing. The problems swirled in ever-increasing circles. The swish of the door interrupted her thoughts as Evelyn exited the office. With a challenging stare, 'Your clothes are too dark. You've only a few luminous straps and the route through the woods will be pitch black.'

Evelyn twisted her head away. 'I've lights and it is a quiet road compared to the main routes.'

'It's not that part of the ride which concerns me, it's after you leave me, you take the roads out of town and towards the motorway and then unlit roads.'

Evelyn didn't reply and yanked open the outside door. Sadie's shoulders slumped as no matter what approach she tried, Evelyn didn't want to be friends. Even persuading her to cycle part of the way home together had been difficult to achieve. While admiring Evelyn's intellect and her remarkable programming skills, if they'd been friends, she would have helped Sadie develop the code for Dess without the others knowing.

They plodded along the concrete walkway in silence to the back of the building and Evelyn unlocked the gate to the bike shelter. As Sadie pulled her bike out and made herself comfortable on the saddle, Evelyn, always slower to mount her bike, rearranged her anorak.

'There are narrow lanes without pavements at the end of your route.' She guessed, as Evelyn had never been forthcoming about where she lived and had determined the general area from her comments, but the exact location remained vague.

'I'm careful.' Her flat tone signalled the end of the conversation. Evelyn pushed on the pedals and they set off. The drone of the motorway hovered in the background.

The mist clung to the face as they cycled past the office blocks, turned across the main road and past the Manor Hotel. The mist changed to a thick fog which swirled eerily in the glow from the streetlamps as they pedalled along the puddle filled road.

Head bent; she pushed hard against the pedals. The lights from other bicycles flickered in the swirls. Their speed increased, making Sadie's face tingle with icy moisture. She would not speak until she had caught her breath.

Warmed from the exertion, her breathing had settled to a regular pattern. Slowing, she waited for Evelyn to catch her. 'I'm so excited that we have the funding. Each of us can develop our own ideas. Aaron mentioned employing more people so we would manage our own team. That's brill! Are you pleased?'

'Yes, I am, as I'm over my initial disappointment, so I'm looking forward to progressing the work.' She did her best to glance across at Evelyn to examine her facial expression, but she'd pulled a scarf up and only her eyes showed and they were firmly focused on the route ahead.

As they left the track, 'What disappointment?'

'Aaron told me in the interview that he would appoint four people and then decide who would be the team leader.' Her voice was muffled by the scarf across her mouth, but she detected a harsh edge to her words. She pedalled on, mulling over the revelation, as Evelyn had never mentioned the conversation with Aaron before.

Unsure of the implication of Evelyn's words, 'I arrived last, so I didn't expect to be in charge.'

'Aaron annoyed me when he chose Simon.' There was no mistaking the curt, strained tone of her voice. Evelyn rarely expressed such forthright views. Normally, her language and words were neutral and non-committal.

Curiosity bubbled up but holding a serious conversation while cycling when she couldn't see Evelyn's face became impossible. With determination and a bit of quick thinking, she slowed her bike and shouted across. 'Can we stop a minute as my helmet strap has come loose?'

She unclicked the strap on her helmet before coming to a halt. Removing her gloves, she fiddled with the straps, pretending to adjust them. 'Did you expect to be picked as team leader?'

'Yes. I'm better qualified than Simon.' Evelyn averted her eyes and lowered her head. 'Haven't you noticed his knowledge can be superficial?' The arrogance of the words made her shudder. This evening, she had seen a different side to Evelyn. Her sudden stringent views must result from the announcement today. Perhaps that is why she spent so long on a private chat with Aaron.

She continued to fiddle with the straps of her helmet. This conversation could become interesting. 'I like Simon. He's a good man. Don't you agree?'

'No,' came the immediate and abrupt reply.

She ventured her own opinion to provoke a reaction. 'Dan is the best, but I like Simon.'

'Dan and you will become an item.' The response surprised her. Perhaps Evelyn would change from the quiet person in the office. She liked people with outspoken views and, as Evelyn was her only female companion, she hoped they could bond.

Candice didn't count as a member of the team, which pleased Sadie because she had never liked her. Wanting Evelyn to lighten, she gave a small, derisive laugh. 'No chance. I'm not into office romances, but under other circumstances, I would go out with Dan. What about you?'

'Not my type.'

She giggled. 'We'll have to have a serious girl's night out so you can tell me about your ideal man.' Evelyn shook her head and pushing on the pedal set off along the track. She clipped on her helmet and pedalled hard to catch Evelyn.

Sadie waved a hand in goodbye as Evelyn rode into the darkness towards her home in Thorpe Hesley. Sighing at the disappointment that they could not establish a friendship, she would complete the social aspects of her project and leave the technical details to someone else.

After a long but exciting day, she pedalled with the enthusiasm her female colleague lacked. Deep in thought about her proposal and the strange reaction from Evelyn on the journey, she nearly missed stopping at a red light in Chapeltown. She took a deep breath, resolving to concentrate on her cycling until she swung into the quiet residential Smith Street where she lived. The ground-floor flat at the end of a Victorian terrace showed a welcoming light in the lounge.

Dess cut across the music from her headphones, 'Nearly home, Sadie. I switched the security lights on earlier.' She smiled. That must have been Dan's work. Automatically she wished to thank Dess, but it was a computer program that didn't need appreciation.

The rear security light came on as she pushed through the back gate to the small yard, where she tucked her bike into a brick outbuilding. The flat suited her. Within easy reach of the centre and while a strain financially to rent it, it allowed the freedom of living on her own as she had no wish to return to her hometown of Bristol and her restrictive parents' house. She shuddered to herself as she recalled the acrimonious arguments which had led to her being thrown out.

Opening the kitchen back door, the warmth of the flat greeted her. The smell of the vegetable casserole in the slow cooker remained strong, but it would have switched off many hours ago. It wouldn't require much effort to re-heat. She hung her cycling clothes on the back door and strolled through to the equally warm lounge with subdued up lighting that came on as she entered.

A gentle voice came from the sound bar. 'Welcome home. Have you had a good day?'

'Hello, Dess. You tell me.' Flopping into the armchair, she stretched her legs out in front of her. Having a conversation with a machine amused her and brought a smile.

'The sentence is too short. I need you to speak to me. Tell me what happened today. Did you win the competition?'

'We all won. Four projects will go forward.'

'That's good news but I can detect stress in your voice.'

Dess had become far more perceptive than any human. 'I'm upset with Evelyn as she is so insular and not friendly.'

'Upset?'

'Yes, I make an approach to be friendly, but she rebuffs me every time.'

'How does she rebuff you?'

'By silence, she doesn't respond. This evening when I asked her about men she rode off.'

'Your day seemed positive, so why let it be overwhelmed by the negativity from Evelyn.'

'You're right Dess. I shall follow your advice. What time did the slow cooker finish?'

'Three thirty this afternoon, but I can switch it back on for you.'

'No thanks, Dess. Next time I use a slow cooker, can you restart it when I leave work.'

'Gotcha. Have a good evening, your anxiety is calming.'

She giggled at the comforting words from the machine as she went to re-heat the casserole, a mindless task that suited her this evening. A good meal and relaxing music, followed by a decadent bath with candles before bed. She might treat herself to a joint. She rarely had them these days, but a little escapism this evening would do no harm.

08

Dan scratched his beard as he peered with intense concentration at the screen. The heady good news of yesterday's decision to progress all projects had evolved into a more sombre atmosphere during the day as the enormity of the task that lay ahead enveloped them.

Hard work beckoned for the next few months. As usual, Evelyn hadn't shared her reaction to the news, but during the day, it had become obvious that Sadie and Simon were feeling the pressure. The unsmiling faces and silence had given them away. There had been no table tennis.

The office in the evening would be his most constructive work time. Peace and quiet with nobody to distract him. A few hours of solid work would build his confidence and, hopefully, he could make progress. When Aaron announced that his project had been selected, amazement had swept through him, closely followed by excitement.

The year had sprung many surprises, especially being employed at TechMatt. Such jobs were like gold dust because they were so popular with graduates. Working for a massive multi-national threatened a long haul up the promotion tree, but start-ups had the potential for money fast and with his debts, that is what he needed.

Taking a swig of Red Bull, he hoped the increased charge of caffeine would keep him alert throughout the evening. Getting this job had been beyond his wildest dreams. His Uni results hadn't been good, but they came as no surprise as he spent his time playing computer games and socialising.

Skipping lectures and handing in skimpy assignments at the last minute had been the norm. He'd had fun, but his debts had ramped up and he'd only just managed to scrape through his degree. How he wished he'd attended his lectures, as his knowledge in many areas of computing had no depth, but it was his own fault.

Pushing the thoughts aside, he focused on the present. Apart from the worry about this project, the relationships in the office had become a concern. He liked Sadie, as her enthusiasm and spontaneity always brought a smile to his face. Evelyn was different, but she caught his attention, although he tried not to show it. What thoughts and ideas swirled behind those searching chocolate brown eyes? Rarely joining in office conversations, she kept her distance.

Whenever possible, he studied her and had fantasised about her. He guessed she would be out of his class, but luck had favoured him recently, so why not ask her out and see what happens? A rush of heat ran over his body. A smile creased his face. Enough daydreaming. He had to stop thinking about Evelyn.

Remembering she'd intended having a quiet night in, he felt guilty about spying on her as he activated the monitors that he'd given her. It had been a pity she didn't want him to visit her flat to fit them, but she had installed them herself. He had agreed on no cameras, but the movement detectors revealed her to be in the lounge. That set his mind whirling. He knew nothing about her. Did she live on her own? Did she have a current boyfriend?

Whenever anyone asked her a personal question, she shrugged and remained silent. Why? Did she have a secret? He had one more check of the monitors; she had moved to the hall, so he waited and kept checking, but there was no further information. Closing her monitoring system, he tried to banish thoughts of Evelyn from his head.

The others would be jumpy and uncooperative if he revealed how much he monitored. To disguise his intentions, he'd packed the monitoring equipment in boxes that he'd designed and built himself. Picking up patterns of behaviour would allow the intelligence of his system to anticipate and provide solutions before being asked.

A noise made him jump. He held his breath and listened. Candice entered the office. Dan began typing, as he didn't want to appear too keen. In a flat and weary tone of voice, 'Hello, Candice. What are you doing here?' Stopping typing, he glanced in her direction.

She posed in the doorway as a smile flickered on her painted lips. Dressed in a pink jacket with matching trousers, the blue blouse provided the contrast and matched the tone of her heeled shoes. Her elegance, coupled with the spellbinding blue eyes and blonde hair, created an alluring picture. Advancing with long fluid steps towards Dan, her hips swayed. The high heels clicked relentlessly on the laminate floor. She pushed her hand through her blonde hair and, with a brooding expression, stopped next to his desk.

'I left something behind yesterday, so I've popped in to pick it up, although it's none of your business.' Tilting her head to one side, she drew in a deep exasperated breath.

'Oooh, we're touchy tonight.' Giving a loud scoffing laugh. 'You weren't like that last week.'

Screwing her eyes, her pretty mouth twisted into a sneer. 'I'd had far too much to drink at the charity evening and you took advantage after taking me home.'

'You seemed keen at the time.'

'Spoken by a true gentleman.' She raised her head, twisted on her heels and strutted towards Aaron's office.

'He's not in.' The comment stated the obvious, as no lights shone through the glazed door.

'Aaron told me he had important business to attend to this evening.'

He raised his eyebrows, but Candice reached for the door handle and wasn't looking at him.

'Do you know where he is?'

'Business,' She had a cool edge to her voice as she flicked on the lights and disappeared into Aaron's office.

Stumbling to his feet, pulling up his jeans, he followed her. He leaned on the door frame. 'You're checking up on him.'

'Don't be so ridiculous, I'm not.' Her voice held an edge, and the response had come too quickly. Picking up a small item from the desk, she made a show of placing it in her bag.

Her action was just a pretense. So, she is checking up on him. 'I enjoyed last week.' He flashed a grin at her. 'Sorry about my snarky remark. I'm discreet. No one else will know.'

Candice flounced toward him and swung her bag onto her shoulder. She came to stand close, 'Let's keep it to ourselves, as we can receive serious money from this business. Let's have harmony in the office.'

The intense smell of her perfume wafted over him. Leaning forward, he kissed her lightly on the lips. She didn't move, so he took a small step and moved his head closer, enjoying the taste of her lips. His thumb caressed her cheek and his breathing quickened. Her lips moved sensuously in response to his and her eyelids fluttered shut.

He moved his hand from her cheek to the back of her head, pulling her closer to deepen the kiss. She moved slightly away, so his hand slipped from her shoulder, down her arm and onto her breast. With a small moan, she pulled her head back and broke the kiss. She rested her forehead against his and her warm breath caressed his face.

'I enjoyed it as well,' she whispered in his ear, 'but it won't be repeated.'

'What! Never!' groaned Dan as his squeeze tightened.

She stepped away from him and his hand dropped, her expression serious. 'Keep our little fling to yourself and create harmony in the office.'

A hopeful frown drew his eyebrows together, 'So sometime in the future.'

She stepped away, 'Of course.' She smiled, and a hint of arrogance glimmered in her eyes.

He followed her to the main office and gave a throaty little laugh which made her glance back. 'What's so funny.'

'Would you like to know where he is?'

'No,' she tossed her head with disdain, 'Aaron's my husband.'

Returning to his computer, he searched through the active icons on his screen. He found what he wanted and leaned back with satisfaction as he waited for Candice to join him.

She had rested her bag on the desk and, with head bent, searched through its contents. If she wasn't interested, she would have left the office. 'You're winding me up. Why would

Aaron tell you?'

Dan grinned. 'He wouldn't, but as part of my project I'm monitoring his car.'

'He would never give you his passwords and certainly not to his Ziani.'

'Candice. Don't forget I control and monitor the cameras in this office, it's surprising what you can see when they are set to magnification.'

A grin spread across her face. 'I supported you in the funding meeting so perhaps you'd better demonstrate your proposal.'

Dan grinned with pleasure as he brought up the information on the screen. 'There you are,' he pointed, 'Perfectly positioned on Google Maps. His car is at a hotel in Donny.'

09

Sadie removed her cycling helmet as she entered the office. The first glimmer of dawn wouldn't appear for another hour. After a fretful night, she resolved to put in the long hours that would be necessary to change her flaky prototype into a robust system.

'Good morning again, Sadie.' The computerised voice filled the office. 'Good journey to work?' The previous evening, she had resolved not to respond to Dess's chat. Even though she'd invented the system, talking to a machine made her uncomfortable as it bordered on insanity. The familiarity and ease of the conversation was too tempting to react as though it were a person. A shiver of pride ran through her at the success she had achieved. Using open-source modules, she had built an effective but flaky system.

Today, her efforts would be focused on finding deficiencies and correcting them. She ignored Dess's conversational mode, 'Any messages for me.'

'Dan left you a message while you were cycling into the office. He worked late and has scandal for you.'

She laughed, 'Tell him I'm not interested.' Dan? A picture of him appeared in her mind. Unruly ginger hair and beard, twinkling eyes and a mischievous grin. A smile crinkled her mouth. What did she think of him? She recalled Evelyn's remark about them becoming an item. Strange because the beer swilling types weren't her normal taste, but he had developed into a great colleague. He had been easy to talk to and had helped with technical issues in her proposal. He appeared keen on her, but then the interest drifted away. Was that her fault, or was he interested in someone else? He had focused on Evelyn frequently.

While unravelling her thoughts of Dan, she stared out of the window. What is different about him? Many of his attributes appealed. She enjoyed his company and he made her laugh. Then a wicked thought crossed her mind and she grinned. He's a good programmer. That had been obvious from the start. Making a success of her project would be easier with Dan's support. Should she consider becoming closer to him? Aaron, Simon, and Evelyn would be awkward about an office affair, but if the business became successful, and the money rolled in, would they care about relationships?

She headed to the kitchen for a fix of herbal tea. As she passed Evelyn's desk, a glistening object on the floor caught her eye. It lay near the back leg of the desk where the cables from the electronic equipment vanished under the floor. It looked familiar. She stopped, stooped, and peered hard.

Was it the bracelet that had mysteriously disappeared from her desk the previous week? She'd left it there by mistake one night, but when she'd come in the following morning, it had gone. It was one of her favourite pieces given to her by a former boyfriend. The simple band had a mixture of her favourite colours, blue and green. She had hunted for the bracelet, but to no avail. The others in the office had helped with the search, but they didn't find it. So why is it on the floor under Evelyn's desk? Relief and surprise that it had been found flooded through her, but as she stooped to climb under the desk, Evelyn's screen flashed into life.

Jumping, she froze to the spot as Evelyn's back view came on the screen. The picture, a replica of the office, as though she sat at the desk. Sadie's breathing quickened as it seemed lifelike. She stared at the image in horror, but then realisation dawned and she recognised it to be an avatar. Why had Evelyn created a realistic screen for herself? That had never been in the proposals.

'May I help you, Sadie?' The avatar's sound echoed in the empty office.

Dess responded, 'There is a strange voice in the office. I thought you were on your own, Sadie.' Her eyes were fixed on the avatar, but she needed to respond to Dess as it had been programmed to raise alarms in personal protection mode. She had set it for cycling to work and hadn't switched it off, knowing it would transfer automatically as soon as it detected a familiar voice in the office. It wouldn't recognise the tinny voice of the avatar.

'It's okay, Dess, it's only an avatar of Evelyn.'

'I'll keep in listening mode.'

The initial surprise had disappeared, though tension gripped her. The avatar was a computer simulation, albeit a clever one, though it was unnerving.

She stepped towards the desk. 'Keep away!'

'Don't be so ridiculous!' she shouted at the image on the screen. A slight movement made her spin around. Evelyn stood behind her with her hands on her hips and an irritated scowl on her face. She jumped and her hand flew to her mouth as she squealed in surprise. 'Where did you come from? I didn't hear the door open.' She pointed a shaking finger towards the screen. 'That avatar frightened the life out of me.'

Evelyn gave Sadie a contemptuous stare, then focused her attention on the avatar. 'It only comes on if someone approaches my desk. I built it a long time ago but modified it when I took the job here. I leave it switched on.' Evelyn's eyes narrowed as she looked her up and down with an air of arrogance. 'Do you want something from my desk? There is only a pad of paper, a pen and my computer.'

Evelyn stepped between her and the desk so with little room, she had no option but to step back. Evelyn's direct approach hadn't altered her determination to investigate the shiny object on the floor. 'Last week I lost my bracelet, I noticed it under your desk, so I intended to pick it up.'

The rapid movement from Evelyn took her by surprise. In one swift movement, she crouched under the desk. The drawers on one side of the desk blocked Sadie's view. Dropping to her hands and knees Evelyn scrabbled around, 'There's nothing here,' her muffled voice shouted from under the desk, 'only the cables going into the floor, it must have been the reflection of them.'

'No, I'm sure you are mistaken,' her voice croaked with emotion. 'It wasn't a cable that caught my attention, it was my bracelet.'

Evelyn scrambled from under the desk, rubbing the dust

from her black trousers. 'There.' She pointed to the dark area beneath the desk. 'I tidied the cables while I was down there.'

She peered around Evelyn's legs. Stepping aside, Evelyn waved her arm towards the carpet. 'Investigate for yourself if you don't believe me.' She wouldn't be defeated, although the area showed only carpet. Nothing sparkled. Dropping to her knees, she shuffled under the desk and pressed her finger in the small gap around the cables.

With extreme concentration she poked around, hoping to feel the metal of the bracelet. Disappointment gripped her. She found nothing. Finally, she wriggled out and regained her feet.

Evelyn folded her arms across her chest. 'You don't believe me, but I only found cables.' Sadie pushed a hand through her hair and grimaced. 'Don't you accuse me have having your bracelet.' Evelyn's raised voice matched the hardness of her penetrating gaze.

It hadn't been a good start to the morning. She shrugged and stomped across to her desk, muttering 'Bitch,' under her breath. The bracelet had been there. She'd seen it. What had Evelyn done with it? The word mysterious jumped into her mind. Should she go to Aaron to explain? Certainty rifled through her mind, but he had more important issues. She couldn't disrupt the working of the business, but Evelyn gave her concern.

10

Aaron, deep in thought, drove along the A61 into Sheffield in the crawl of traffic headed for the town centre ring road. The ponderous journey gave him time to reflect as he switched his Ziani into traffic aware cruise control. Holding lightly onto the steering wheel, his mind trawled back through the events of the day without having to worry if he lost concentration on the car in front as his car would drift to a halt.

While hard work beckoned for them over the next few months, today the atmosphere in the office had changed and not in the way he expected. Judging by the body language, Sadie had argued with Evelyn, but no one was prepared to speak to him. Simon had evaded the matter and fobbed him off with an inane comment about pressure of work.

Did Simon have his finger on the pulse in the office or would it be better to replace him as team leader? A frosty attitude existed between Sadie and Evelyn, although they had never been friendly. He hadn't managed to speak to Evelyn apart from a few minutes of private conversation during which his priority was to meet again outside of work and not ruin his chances by asking about Sadie.

The first meeting with Evelyn had been successful, she'd relaxed and they had enjoyed each other's company. A pleasurable tingle ran through his body. A smile came as he approached the gates on the drive of his home in Fulwood. Evelyn had been keen to express her views. Ambitious, she wanted to be placed in charge of the expanded project. He would have to consider her role, but he wouldn't decide until the liaison fizzled out.

Seducing Evelyn would be his desire, but he wouldn't rush, although the signs he had received by the touching and close personal presence suggested he would succeed, although he had to be careful that it didn't upset the equilibrium of the project.

The electricity between them had left him wanting more. Infatuation, desire and lust surged through him. With reluctance, he pushed the thoughts aside. The gates across the drive recognised his car, which paused momentarily as they automatically opened. The Ziani swung onto the loose gravel and came to a halt in front of the house.

The wind blew as he stepped from his car; he shivered as it bit through his thin cashmere jumper. The growl of the tree and the overhanging branches swayed alarmingly in the near gale force eddies. The movement of the bushes near the security lights caused a flickering of the brightness as it spread out from the house towards the garage. Pressing his mobile, he trotted towards the front door of the house. The light in the main bedroom told him that Candice was at home. As he reached the front door, he heard the garage door open and the crunch of the tyres on the gravel as the car slowly edged forward to park itself inside.

Unlocking the Yale, he stepped into the warmth of the hall. A small red light on the unit attached to the back of the door caught his eye as he closed it behind him. One of Dan's devices. He made a mental note to check with Dan about the nature of the recordings. He guessed the opening and closing of the front door was being monitored. Although doubtful about its usefulness, he supposed that for some people and businesses, it might be relevant. He must talk to Dan about keyless entry systems, as they seemed to be the way forward.

He picked up the day's post from the hall table, glanced at the envelopes and stuffed them in the drawer without opening them. 'Hello, darling.' Candice came down the stairs.

He smiled, but it dropped away as she had dressed to go out. The cream single button jacket and straight legged navy-blue trousers with sharp creases were new and exuded class. The matching cream strappy high heels waited for her at the bottom of the stairs. Kissing him on the cheek, she bent down to slip into her shoes.

'Are you going out again?' His voice sounded tired and had an edge of irritation. The stress of arranging the financial backing had made life difficult even though it came from his friend Ahmed. He and the team had worked many late nights ensuring that the best proposals were presented to the decision meeting of Ahmed and his friends. He wanted a quiet night in with Candice, as she had been out most evenings in the past month.

She stood in front of the large ornate hall mirror and tweaked her hair into place. Then with practiced ease, she applied her lipstick. An attractive woman who chose her clothes with care to enhance her slim and elegant figure. He forced a smile and leaned towards her, touching her lightly on the arm as he didn't want her to go out this evening.

'I've arranged to meet the girls, it's Katie's birthday. She doesn't want a great fuss, only a meal.'

'I wanted to talk to you this evening,' he persisted, hoping that she might change her mind.

'Is it about the new project?'

'Yes,' his teeth clenched in frustration around the single word. He wanted Candice to be more regularly involved in the new business venture or leave it entirely to him rather than flit in and out, depending on her mood and social commitments.

Candice bent down, unclipped her shoes, and slid her feet out. 'I've time, darling,' her voice softened, she gave a wide smile displaying her perfect white teeth. 'I wanted to go early because it's a problem getting a taxi in the middle of the evening.'

He studied her carefully but didn't move. Something in her manner caught his attention, though he couldn't put his finger on it.

'Where are you meeting Katie?'

'At the Ecclesall Gym,' she pouted her lips at him. 'It's where she does her classes, so we'll go on from there.'

The doubts resurfaced. There was something puzzling about her manner this evening. Uncertainty gripped him. Simon had mentioned earlier today that he intended to visit the Ecclesall Gym. About a month ago, he had enrolled and enjoyed his new meditation classes. He believed the ideas helped him concentrate on work.

The meeting, when all four proposals were considered,

flashed to the forefront of his mind. In the debate about whose project should go forward, Candice had been adamant that Simon's had been the best proposal. His mind drifted to when they had appointed the team leader. Initially, he had chosen Evelyn because of her qualifications, but Candice became insistent about Simon.

He paused; it wouldn't be the first time. Then a flush of guilt flared up as he hadn't been the most faithful of husbands.

Her soft voice jerked him back to reality. 'You're daydreaming darling. Is the stress of work distracting you?' He shook his head. 'If it's urgent we can talk, then I'll take a chance with a taxi.'

Aaron wanted to talk to her about problems the business faced. Sometimes she thought of another way of tackling an issue, even though she didn't understand the technology. A plan formed in his mind. 'We won't risk you being delayed so I'll drop you off and we can talk on the way.' He leaned against the newel post, pleased with his idea.

'There's no need for you to take me, Aaron. I'm not keen on drinking tonight so I can take my car.'

Why be so awkward? He had suggested a perfect solution. He smiled and kissed her on the cheek, 'No arguments, darling.'

'We will get stuck in the traffic along the Ecclesall Road,' she persisted as her mouth tensed and she pressed her lips together.

'That doesn't matter, we can talk on the way and you won't be late arriving. Now pop your shoes on and I'll summon the car.'

His voice had an authoritative tone, which would quell further protests. A double plan formed in his mind and a twist of pleasure fluttered. As Candice intended meeting friends, he could return to the office where Evelyn would be working late.

Candice glanced at her jewelled watch, looked at his face and complied with his instructions. Grabbing a jacket from the hall cupboard, he pressed summon on his mobile phone. Candice shivered in her thin jacket as they left the house. Aaron, without looking at her, smiled, as she would always go for fashion over comfort. The garage door rose and clicked fully open.

The car emerged from the garage and swung in front of him. Opening the passenger's door for Candice, he pulled his jacket tight against the wind and nipped to the driver's door. As he typed the name of the gym into the web browser, it appeared after a few letters so had already been added to the destination list for the satnav. Candice must have visited before in his car to meet Katie. Pressing the confirm button, he selected autopilot and auto-navigate and relaxed in the driving seat.

Keeping a light touch on the steering wheel, he allowed the car to manoeuvre as it set off on its course. The gates closed automatically behind them with a loud clunk.

Candice selected soft background music and relaxed back on the white leather seats. 'What did you want to tell me, darling?'

Confident that the car would navigate and control their progress, he twisted to face her. Her reaction would show on her face even if the words did not match. 'I had a meeting with Ahmed today. We demonstrated Dess to his financial friends and they are willing to invest the full amount.'

'That's brilliant news, darling.' Her voice bubbled and her eyes sparkled in the dim light. 'That will make future growth much easier.' Candice had a knack for finding the right words.

'It will, but they want the software quickly. Ahmed's investors anticipate a great opportunity, but we need to deliver in a short timescale. The giant IT organisations will take longer to reach market, so the investors want our products as the market leader.'

'Do they still want the triangle of Dan, Sadie and Simon's proposal?'

'Yes, with Evelyn's given a good prominence in the background.'

The car halted in traffic and edged forward, but neither took notice. Candice stared at the bright red lights from the cars ahead as they moved along the Ecclesall Road. 'Can the team produce the results in the timescale?'

Once again, a perceptive question from Candice. 'The moneymen want us to increase the size of the team and move to larger premises.' A hint of a frown appeared on his face.

'Why the serious expression? Surely that's good news.'

'Yes,' he pressed his lips firmly together, 'but there is a problem. One of Ahmed's friends is a technology specialist. He wanted to examine the CVs of the team, so I sent them for his perusal. He believes they are too inexperienced. The move to new premises could bring in fresh staff with a higher level of expertise. But he has agreed to meet one of them and make up his mind.'

'I can appreciate his point, but what about the existing team?' She fixed her anxious gaze on his face. 'Won't they leave and take their ideas elsewhere?'

'Ahmed wants me to keep the same team but with a substantial rise in salary, then develop the ideas quickly. The second phase wouldn't need them.'

'Sounds risky to me,' Candice pressed her lips firmly together, emphasising her disapproval.

'I agree.' He rubbed a hand across his face. 'And to add to the problem, Evelyn is threatening to leave.'

'Why?'

'She's upset at not being the team leader and I've the impression that unless she takes charge she will search for another job.'

'What about Simon?'

'He's settled, but if I give the leadership to someone else, I can't anticipate his reaction.'

Candice jerked her head up. 'You must keep Simon. He can keep the team together.'

Studying her face, no hidden meaning showed. 'We're here, darling,' he announced with a wave of his arm as the car turned into the gym car park.

'Shall we have a coffee? I can stay until Katie arrives.' Without waiting for an answer, he leapt out of the car and whizzed to open the passenger door. He strolled arm in arm with Candice to the door of the gym.

'No, darling. You've had a busy day. Go home and rest.' She rested her hands on his shoulder with a concerned expression on her face.

'Okay. If you're sure.' He kissed Candice lightly on the lips and returned to his car. A wave of concern coursed through him. Had he made the right decision? He glanced back towards the gym entrance. Should he pop back and talk to Candice until Katie arrived? It would set his mind at rest. Or should he find Evelyn? He scratched the stubble on his chin while indecision gripped him.

Neither would be a good move. He typed in his golf club where he could relax with a meal and would find another member to join for a drink.

11

Candice fidgeted on her seat in the café-bar area. The groups of four low backed chairs in the bright red upholstery were centred around circular coffee tables. The smell of food and drinks from the serving counter mixed with the slight waft of chlorine when the door to the pool opened.

Why had Aaron wanted to drive her to the gym, his insistence was out of character? The discussion had been mundane and did not require disruption to the evening. Did he have another agenda? Perhaps he doubted her fidelity. It wouldn't be the first time, but his accusations normally wavered as she confronted him about his behaviour. Shuffling again, she would have to make a judgement about the evening.

As he hadn't returned on a trumped-up excuse, she looked up after studying the contents of her handbag. 'Hello, Simon. Fancy meeting you here.' After sipping from her mineral water, she gave a delicate smile towards Simon but didn't stand up.

Simon's forehead creased as a quizzical expression flitted across his face. Then understanding dawned and he glanced around.

Hopefully, he'd guessed that Aaron might be here. While she had looked forward to the private conversation, the evening's attitude from Aaron had made her wary. Simon's smart black chinos and a pale blue polo neck top highlighted his torso. The light, casual, soft black shoes added to his smartness. His short brown hair had been stylishly cut. She liked a man who had tried with his appearance. She groaned to herself. His smartness contrasted to the unkempt and wild image of Dan which had popped unbidden into her mind.

What had possessed her after the charity dinner? Dan's seduction of her, while enjoyable, must not be repeated. She would endeavour to remove him from the business to ensure he didn't blab. Simon would be different, as he would be discreet. A frisson of excitement rippled through her and with difficulty, she suppressed a giggle.

In an exaggerated voice, Simon responded, 'Hi, Candice. This is a surprise.' His eyes swept the lounge. 'Is Aaron here?'

'He's dropped me off and could be nearby.' With a stare of suspicion, she gazed towards the entrance. A sudden stab of nervousness hit her. She had agreed to meet Simon in a public place so their meeting wouldn't arouse suspicion. She wanted assurance that before any private meeting he would comply with her wishes.

Simon took the hint, 'I'll walk outside and see if he's there.' He strode across the lounge towards the door, his slim, tall frame moved with lightness and ease. The toned body would be fun to explore. The possibility of Aaron being nearby filled her with concern. Attempting to calm her racing heart, she mulled through a range of contingencies. Katie might appear as she came most nights to the gym after work. Her presence would be helpful if Aaron returned, or Simon would not agree to abide by her rules.

Within a few minutes, he returned with a wide grin on his face. 'His Ziani pulled out of the car park.' He eased himself onto the adjacent chair and stretched his long legs out in front of him.

'It's too risky to stay long.' Her voice was edged with tension.

'Okay, so come back to my place.' He touched her arm. 'It's not far?'

'Not tonight, Simon.' A flush of colour warmed her cheeks. 'Aaron is over attentive. He'll be away in France next week. Let's meet then.' Simon folded his arms across his chest, while an expression of discontent furrowed his forehead. 'Don't be awkward.' Her heartbeat quickened with apprehension. 'We can enjoy ourselves but need to be confident that no one will discover our meetings. I guessed you live nearby. Coming to your place would make me nervous. Let's meet at a hotel.'

'Okay,' he spoke the single word in a low pained voice. Her tension eased now that she'd sorted the arrangements to her satisfaction. Simon might be disappointed about tonight, but Aaron had been in a strange mood for the past week. He kept changing his mind, which makes him unpredictable. Aaron rarely asked where she'd been or what her plans were for the evenings, but his new attentiveness rattled her nerves.

Once the new funding had settled down, he'd be back to normal and then she would discreetly meet Simon. An evening with him filled her with anticipated pleasure. Perhaps new sexy underwear was needed before the clandestine liaison took place. The idea of shopping cheered her up.

With an effort, she focused her thoughts back on the present. 'Text me Monday morning after he's gone.' Her tone brooked no negotiation.

Simon nodded twice, saying nothing, staring down towards his outstretched feet. Candice offered him the bottle she'd been drinking from. He took a sip. Smiling apologetically, she opened her bag and took out a tissue. 'You've picked up lipstick.'

Leaning close so the fragrance of her floral perfume drifted across him, she smiled and gently wiped his bottom lip. His eyes flashed. 'That's better. I like it when you smile.' Candice stood up. 'Come on, let's stand in reception. There's a person who has arrived in the lounge who I want to avoid.'

Simon uncoiled himself from the low chair and followed her to the side of reception. Candice stood away from the automatic double glass doors. The windy drafts, from them repeatedly opening, made reception chilly. She studied him, 'I've bad news for you, but you need to know.'

'What is it?' His eyes widened in alarm.

'Ahmed and his friends want to replace you as team leader. They want a more experienced person in charge.'

His posture stiffened. 'So, I'm being undermined by my team and pressurised by the money men.'

She picked up the implied disharmony with his colleagues. 'Tell me more. What's wrong with the team?'

'Evelyn is close to Aaron. Whenever he comes out of his office, it's always to speak to her. It's never me.' He shifted his weight from foot to foot and gave a tight-lipped smile. 'Also,

Sadie and Evelyn must have had an argument. Neither would speak about it, but Sadie's eyes followed Evelyn's every move. Work progress is minimal.' He breathed heavily. 'It held the prospects of a good job when I started with Aaron but perhaps it's time to move on. I'm considering setting up on my own. My idea will work and then I can keep the money.'

'But I don't want you to leave.' She brushed him gently on the arm and her cheeks flushed. 'We're just getting together.'

He drew in a large breath and released it before speaking. 'While I like you, it's not much fun waiting. We spoke about meeting several weeks ago and it still hasn't happened.'

She glanced around with an anxious frown. 'I'm sure Aaron's coming back,' her voice wavered, 'Perhaps he's guessed.'

'We can't go on like this Candice, to my mind it is over before we've started.' Squaring his shoulders, he stared at her through narrowed eyes.

She understood his annoyance. The fault lay with her as she'd kept postponing the meeting. Anxiety and uncertainty overwhelmed her. She cast a frightened glance over her shoulder, half expecting to see Aaron striding angrily towards her. Her skin prickled with nervousness. Should she start an affair with Simon? Aaron was becoming suspicious and she wanted to keep her indiscretions away from him.

The thunderous expression on Simon's face showed his focus had returned to the problems of work. 'Who wants me out? That's more important than you and me. Is it that Ahmed?'

'He leads the consortium and he has people spare from another investment that is ending.'

'How do you know that?' The accusation in his narrowed eyes showed suspicion.

'Calm down, I've known him for years.' She didn't add that they had been lovers at one time. 'He has been a friend of Aaron's since they worked together in the city.' Simon twisted away in readiness to leave. 'Are you going?'

'Yes,' he muttered with a dismissive wave of his hand, 'I need to consider the various options open to me at work.' She silently admonished herself. Why had she brought up the business? If she met him at a hotel, she'd make sure there was no mention of the project. 'I'll text you on Monday, but my guess is Aaron will postpone his visit to France as it isn't important for the business.' His voice had become crisp and confident. 'If he does, it will mean another delay for us.' He gave a half smile, shrugged and left through the automatic doors.

She stood motionless until his retreating figure disappeared. That's strange. Aaron had said the French visit would be crucial for the business. Why doesn't Simon think the same? What does he know? Suspicion tormented her, but he's not in a receptive mood, so there's no point in going after him.

She retrieved her mobile from her bag, as she'd become convinced Aaron would return to surprise her with some weak excuse. Her face tightened with a frown as her manicured fingers flicked over the apps screen of her mobile. She pressed the Ziani symbol and waited for the app to connect to the car. Raising her eyebrows with a mixture of surprise and confusion as the app showed the car parked at the golf club. She'd anticipated wrongly. Perhaps the stress of the business had triggered his unpredictable behaviour. Hopefully, he didn't harbour suspicions about her.

Candice took a deep breath and relaxed. Simon would present her no problems. Although she had not responded well, with the right lingerie she could entice him and make him forget about their poor start. Aaron had gone to the golf club which had not conformed to his usual pattern. He only ever visited when he wanted a round. While frustrated, at least no disasters or embarrassing situations had arisen.

Her phone pinged with an incoming message. Ahmed wanted her to ring him. She strode across the busy reception and into the lounge bar and settled at a quiet table in the corner but hesitated as her unseeing eyes roamed the room while her hand hovered over the phone. Her mouth had gone dry, and her heart hammered. Ahmed presented a complication she didn't need. Flicking the phone, she would make the call before second thoughts won.

Talking to him wouldn't be a good idea. Holding her breath, she waited. 'What do you want?' she snapped as he answered.

'Did Aaron tell you about the money I offered today?'

Clenching her jaw at the sound of his smooth voice. 'Yes, but I don't understand, you have never been keen on Aaron's business so why become involved.' Her mind raced. 'What's the real reason behind your activities? You're up to something.'

'It's an excuse to see you more often,' his confident voice purred.

She'd expected a devious plan from him. 'It's over Ahmed and has been for a long time.'

He didn't appear dissuaded by her words as he responded without a moment's hesitation, 'I wanted to have another chance to persuade you as I'm buying a yacht.'

She imagined him smiling at the impact his words would cause. 'A new one?' Candice curled her long fingers around the phone and her heart skipped a beat. A yacht had been her dream, but she attempted to organise her thoughts. Did he have that much money?

'Yes, brand new I ordered it over two years ago but didn't tell anyone. The sea trials end next week and they will hand it over to me.' He chuckled with genuine excitement. 'Why not come away with me? Leave Aaron then we can spend the winter cruising the Med.'

Her heart leapt as images of herself lounging on the deck of a luxurious yacht leapt into her mind. Champagne parties. Mixing with the elite and famous. The practicalities of life soon squashed the thoughts into oblivion, 'What about the money you have invested with Aaron?'

'It's only £400k,' he responded in a dismissive tone. 'It's irrelevant if I have you instead.' His words hung in the air. Her breath had become too dry for speech so the silence between them stretched, 'Something has occurred that I hadn't expected.'

Confusion wrinkled her brow as she tried to guess, 'What is it?'

'The consortium is seriously interested in Aaron's business as they like Dess and are prepared to invest substantial money, possibly millions, but they will press for subsequent follow-on ideas.'

Frowning, she clamped the phone to her ear with shaking hands, 'But I'm still involved, so we can see each other. Every time we meet, your hypnotic charm electrifies me, I long to hold you in my arms again.'

Her throat contracted with emotion at his words, her heartbeat quickened. 'No, Ahmed.' Tears rose, but she quelled them, 'I will stick with Aaron. It's not all fun but we struggle through. I'm apprehensive about jumping into a man's bed at any opportunity. Times change and move on; I will stick with Aaron and stop having wandering eyes. Hopefully he will not kick me out.'

'Do you think I would?'

'You have a reputation and it isn't loyalty to your partners. I'm sticking with Aaron.' She gripped the phone with determination. 'He has the odd liaison but soon loses interest, then I make him pay before I forgive him.'

'You're a hard-nosed woman, Candice.' The words came in a low pained voice.

'No, Ahmed, I'm practical in protecting my best interests. I believe he's involved with someone, but it will only be a casual fling.' A lump grew in her throat as Aaron was the man she loved.

'When the money and staff are discussed, I can make sure she leaves the business.' He gave a throaty laugh.

What did Ahmed know? Evelyn's mysterious aura would intrigue Aaron. While Sadie was an attractive young woman, she wouldn't be his type. She preferred to ignore Aaron's wandering and pursue odd ones of her own, but recently she soon became bored with her flirtatious conquests. The time had arrived to amend her ways. Perhaps she might become a dutiful wife who only had eyes for her husband. A silent snort of amusement escaped from her lips. Did she believe that? Tears clouded her blue eyes. This conversation required a change of direction.

'Has Dan or Evelyn ever been in your car or driven it.' He sighed.

'Okay, you want to change the subject. Dan and Evelyn in my car?' A sudden note of confusion crept into his voice. 'No, not that I know. Why do you ask?'

Candice chose her words with care to ensure she came across as the innocent party. 'Dan has been monitoring Aaron's car and he showed me the results on the computer.'

Ahmed's loud yawn travelled down the phone line, 'I expect Aaron gave permission as it's linked to Dan's project.'

'Yes, but a few days later in the evening I popped into the office and Dan sat at Evelyn's desk using her computer as his was backing up. He didn't hear me arrive, so I crept up behind him. The information on the screen seemed obvious even to me. Evelyn had been tracking Zianis. Dan shut it down as soon as he became aware of my presence. However, he wasn't fast enough.'

'Probably the same project, nothing unusual. They share ideas and information between the four, don't they? Dan passed a copy to Evelyn. Normal practice I would say?' His tone became dismissive.

Raising her eyes to the ceiling, scorn flashed across her face. He won't be so flippant when he finds out the whole story, so she pressed on with her explanation. 'I questioned him. It wasn't his project and he had come across it while monitoring Evelyn's technology and had become inquisitive.'

'What's that to me?'

A smile twitched at her lips. For an intelligent man he was slow to grasp the obvious implication. 'There were two Zianis on the screen.' Explaining patiently, she suppressed a bubble of laughter.

'Could be anyone.'

Allowing the pause to lengthen, she held her breath before divulging the last piece of information. 'On Monday night about eight in the evening, were you in the centre of Milton Keynes?'

A long silence but she waited, while nerves fluttered in the pit of her stomach.

'Yes.' The single word flashed down the phone. 'This has become serious. We ought to meet.'

'Yes, I agree but I'm making no promises.'

Giving a gruff laugh, 'That's okay, but let's keep this information to ourselves.'

'Yes, that would be best.' She disconnected the call.

12

Dan had finally persuaded Sadie to join him for an after work drink. He had pestered her, but until tonight she had never yielded. He liked to relax with a pint after work, especially in the company of a good-looking woman. His social contacts had dwindled because of working late most evenings, but he viewed it as a positive as he could clear his new debts and focus on his career rather than wasting his time on rugby, beer and computer games.

Strolling into the subdued lighting of the Manor bar, the dark stained wood and the thick upholstery gave a traditional feeling. He would always feel comfortable in such surroundings and disliked modern brightly lit bars with uncomfortable seats, accompanied by loud music.

They had walked the short distance across the hazardous main road to the quiet and comfort of the bar and installed themselves in the corner behind a glazed screen. Wriggling his large frame into a comfortable position, he grinned at Sadie. 'It's a pleasant surprise that you finally agreed to come for a drink with me.'

'I only came because I didn't ride my bike today and you've been nagging me for a drink.' Her eyes flashed. 'The bike had a puncture this morning, so I travelled on the bus. It's a quick drink after work with a colleague, nothing more. Then I will call a taxi. Is that understood?'

A furrow of confusion wrinkled Dan's brow. Why is she so defensive, as I only asked her for a drink? A barman drifted towards them and took their order for a pint of Carlsberg and a small Chardonnay.

Being direct would be his only approach. 'Is it because we work together that you won't date me?'

'Yes.' Shifting her eyes towards a noisy group of suited businessmen that had emerged from a nearby function room, she nodded to confirm her view, 'That's the main reason.'

'Is there another?'

'Yes.' She hesitated as though preparing to say more, but

then changed her mind.

'Go on tell me, I won't take it personally.'

Before she responded, the drinks arrived, allowing her time before replying. 'You only have eyes for Evelyn and although you've no chance, you can't stop watching her. Given your performance, I'm surprised she hasn't complained. I find your attitude to her embarrassing as you're always asking her if she wants a drink, but you never ask Simon or me.'

His cheeks burned red with embarrassment and he took a swig of his beer to hide his face as his mind raced. Did his behaviour appear that obvious? Grimacing, he searched for an excuse. 'She is closest to me and I can't see what you and Simon are doing because of the equipment, so I don't wish to disturb you.'

Lazing back in her chair, she took a large gulp of her white wine. 'I notice you don't deny it.' A note of contempt had crept into her voice. Her attitude had taken Dan by surprise, with her forthright opinion about him and Evelyn. The words hit their mark and he didn't want further unwanted comments.

The challenging approach tonight was unusual, as in the office she chatted and appeared friendly. Her assessing eyes bored into him, so he leaned back in his chair, fighting the irritation which coursed through him at being discovered. Sadie liked to hear the latest gossip, so leaned forward in a conspiratorial manner. 'I never told you the bit of scandal that I found out.'

Leaning back in her chair, she glanced up at the ceiling with an irritated frown. The evening had not developed as he'd expected, his plan had been to have a laugh and a few drinks, but the atmosphere between them had deteriorated. Mulling over his best approach, he gulped down the icy cold lager as he needed to return to Sadie's good books.

Replacing his glass on the table, he gave an exaggerated wink, 'Do you want to know what happened when I stayed in the office late.' She gave no reaction. 'I set my machine to do updating, which would take several hours, so I intended leaving it overnight. Then I remembered earlier work that I hadn't finished, so I moved to Evelyn's desk.'

'Did the avatar tell you off?'

Raising his eyebrows in surprise, 'Yes, it made me laugh, it's good, isn't it?'

'Did it tell you to keep away?'

'Yes.'

'Did you?'

'No, I took no notice of a stupid avatar. I was tempted to substitute a picture of me, but it might disrupt the office and I would get the sack, which I couldn't afford. But it's a bloody silly idea, does she think we are half-wits?'

Showing a neutral expression, with an intense gaze at Sadie, 'I wanted to find information, so I sat at her desk and killed the avatar program. I logged on as the system manager over the network and found my unfinished work.'

She flicked a dismissive hand in his direction. 'That's hardly worth telling.'

'No, that's not the juicy information. I reckoned Evelyn would be annoyed if her avatar had stopped running.'

'Yes,' agreed Sadie, with a glimmer of amusement in her eyes.

'I tried a reboot, but it didn't work.'

'So, what happened?' A smile of eagerness flashed across her face as she leaned towards him.

Taking his time as her face had returned to the normal friendly smile. 'The file names were coded. I'd found the right directory, but nothing leapt out at me. In the end I must have pressed the wrong program because a map came up instead of the avatar.'

Her face crinkled in confusion. 'I don't understand why that's significant.'

'It was a monitoring system for cars which moved in real-time, which is tricky to do. Most of the software for live views is expensive, so why was it hidden on Evelyn's machine?'

'How did you evade the password.'

He touched the side of his nose and winked, 'I have ways and means as the systems manager.'

'Go on.' Her voice and smile had returned to normal.

Taking a swig of his beer as he now had her full concentration. 'There weren't many cars on her system, as they belonged to people in the office.'

'Are you sure? How could you tell?'

Laughing, 'She had them labelled. Ah refers to Ahmed's, and Aa to Aaron's.'

A frown creased her forehead, 'Ahmed told me he didn't want any part of the project as he wouldn't have anyone monitoring what he did.'

'That doesn't surprise me. I hear he chases women all the time and catches many.'

'Ahmed's tried nothing with me.'

'It's obviously not your turn for the swathe of charm.' Again, he laughed.

She pouted. 'Labelling something Ah is hardly definitive. Are you sure you're not making this up, Dan?'

Nodding to the barman as he passed, he ordered two more drinks, then yanked out his mobile phone. 'I'll show you how I know.' He tapped one app. 'This is the monitoring on Aaron's car, he's at the golf club tonight. So, two cars that I know the location are mine and Aaron's. Evelyn's tracker hit spot on with Aa and mine D, so I assumed the others were correct.'

'Tracking of cars is not the project she's working on; you might do it but not her. What's she up to?'

He grinned, 'I'm not sure why she's tracking cars, but I know what she's up to.'

'What are you talking about?'

'Evelyn's car had the label, mine. Aaron's is Aa. They were parked next to each other at a hotel in Doncaster.'

'What time? It's not necessarily significant.'

'Nine o'clock in the evening. I worked a late shift because I'm behind on my plan.'

She giggled, 'I shall have to watch myself, everyone including you will be spying on me.'

His smile disappeared, 'I wanted to examine her machine

to discover what else she monitored about the people in the office.'

'Did you?'

'I didn't have the chance as Candice dropped in.'

'Why so late in the evening?'

He waited. Understanding soon spread across her face and she answered her own question, 'Checking up on Aaron.'

Sadie giggled. 'So, there is an office romance.'

'Romance isn't the word I would use.'

Sadie giggled again, 'The wine is going to my head. I've not eaten all day.'

'Why don't we stay and eat, I'm hungry and we need to chat.'

'Why?' Her eyes narrowed.

'We need to support each other. The work isn't easy, but we can succeed with hard graft.'

'Makes sense, but...'

Holding up his hand. 'We need to be mates at work. Let's get pissed tonight and sort out the world. I won't get heavy with you as I need your help in the office as I'm the weak link.' He passed her the menu.

13

Simon had stomped away from Candice who he had left in the gym reception. Despite the cold wind, he didn't pull his jacket tight. Jumping into his car; he slammed the door and crashed his fist on the dashboard. Nothing had gone according to plan. A hot flush had swept across his cheeks. Without moving he sat until shivering with cold. His mind raced but a solution evaded him. How much time passed while deep in thought he didn't know.

'What shall I do?' he shouted to the confines of the car. A person a few cars away flung his kit bag into the boot. The shouting attracted his attention. Simon faced the front and ignored the man who drove away. The Fitbit buzzed on his wrist. He glanced at his readings, but he didn't care. Flopping back into the driver's seat, he closed his eyes. He tried deep breathing exercises as recommended in his meditation class, but after a few breaths he gave up.

He had been on tenterhooks as he had expected spending the evening with Candice. Little had been achieved with his work that day as his mind wandered through a range of exciting scenarios, each one more breath-taking than the last.

When she had dropped hints a few weeks ago, he'd taken them up immediately. He hadn't had a regular girlfriend for six months. Lethargy had struck him when he couldn't find a job. He couldn't be bothered chasing a woman when he had little money. The last one had dumped him. She'd told him in no uncertain terms exactly what she thought about him before leaving. She had accused him of being far too serious, a workaholic making him boring and no fun to be around. When he started working for Aaron, the job had been demanding, so no new girlfriend had entered his life.

The offer from Candice appeared perfect. Sex without complications. Although about ten years older than him, she had a good figure and he had been waiting patiently to get her into bed. The last few days he'd been cleaning and tidying his flat, expecting a romantic evening with her. A bottle of champagne lay chilling in his fridge. A vase of flowers decorated the coffee table in the lounge. All that effort for nothing.

A flash of annoyance raced through him, followed by disappointment. Leaning forward, he gripped the steering wheel and stared with unseeing eyes through the windscreen. Another empty evening stretched ahead of him. Candice wouldn't happen soon, if at all. Although he suspected from the outset the affair would be short-lived. She had pushed him aside tonight as though superfluous to requirements.

He rubbed his face. A stab of anxiety hit him as his mind spiralled. More important than her rejection of him had been the snippet of news she'd related. She had hinted that his role as team leader would be under threat.

With the many and lengthy chats between Evelyn and Aaron, he guessed at a re-organisation of the team, especially if more employees joined the company. Dan had suggested that Evelyn and Aaron were having an affair. If so, would he promote Evelyn to the team leader role?

Time for action. He would have accepted the decision if Aaron had sacked him because his work didn't reach the required standard, but that wouldn't have mattered if he was going to bed with Candice. Allowing Evelyn to undermine him was unacceptable. Sitting back, awaiting the outcome, didn't present itself as a viable option.

What to do first? Screwing up his eyes, he mindlessly focused on the dark hedge in front of the car. Ideas circled, but indecisiveness gripped him. He breathed slowly, but the Fit-bit continued to buzz. The readings would have to wait. With a flash of irritation, he switched off his watch, snatched it from his wrist and threw it onto the back seat.

The red figures of the clock on the dashboard registered eight o'clock. There was time to act tonight. It couldn't be delayed any longer. An idea formed in his mind, so he slid his phone from his pocket. If Aaron had recently left the gym, he couldn't have reached Evelyn, if that was what he intended this evening.

After a few thumb flicks, he located her number, took a

deep breath and pressed the dial icon. Clutching the phone, he waited for her to answer with bated breath.

'Hello, Simon. Why have you rung, it's late?'

There had been no welcome in her voice, but he hadn't expected it. He bit back his irritation at the implication of it being late. 'I must talk to you. You've been closeted with Aaron most of the day. Can we meet this evening?'

Silence from Evelyn. No sound, just the pounding of his heart as he waited and drummed his fingers on the dashboard. 'No, it's inconvenient.' He stiffened at the curt note in her voice, but he'd expected a fob off.

'Evelyn. This is serious.' He swallowed to ease the dryness in his throat. 'I'm not asking you out as your rejection of me is obvious, but I want to talk about work. Unless we pull together, we will be out of a job, it's that serious.'

The silence made him shuffle in his seat. A hot flush of temper stormed across his cheeks. His fingers wrapped around the steering wheel. Even in the darkness, he observed his knuckles turning white.

'Okay.' Her tone abrupt and contemptuous. 'But only for a short time, I'd planned a night in.'

Did this woman have no sense of urgency, a frown creased his forehead.

'Shall I come to you?'

'No. No.' Her loud, high-pitched response held a hint of fear.

'Name somewhere.' The retort sprang from his lips. He wouldn't be dismissed.

After a brief silence, her voice hissed into his ear, 'TGI Friday's at Meadowhall.'

Simon raised his eyebrows at the choice. 'I'll be there in fifteen minutes.' He closed the call before she changed her mind.

Jamming the car into gear, he screeched out of the car park with unnecessary speed. As he followed the procession of red rear lights along the familiar road, he considered his approach. Tension gripped him and his usual safe driving became erratic. He leaned on the horn, when yet another driver slowed down to let a waiting car into the endless stream of traffic. He had a vice-like grip on the steering wheel. He'd become convinced Evelyn held the key to the success of the business and his job.

A no nonsense approach appeared the best way forward. A stunning woman, but he would ignore her appeal this evening as he wanted to focus on the business and his future. As he parked, Evelyn's car hadn't arrived.

Settling himself on a stool at the counter with a bottle of Bud, his eyes stared with deadly concentration at the door. With one elbow resting on the bar, he barely noticed the crowd of people and the thudding background music. Pushing open the door and with a glance in his direction, she marched across the bar.

The stiff manner warned him she didn't want to meet. No smile appeared on her expressionless face. The solemnness of her manner only increased her mysteriousness. What lay behind those piercing eyes? Would he ever find out? Did she ever let her hair down and have fun?

The black low heeled sensible shoes showed no flamboyance, implying the exact opposite, and would have suited a woman in her fifties. Sheer skin-coloured tights showed her legs and led to a straight black skirt that finished just above her knee. A dark brown jacket, probably vegan leather, completed her appearance. Her hands, with neatly manicured nails but no varnish, appeared cold. She hadn't had time to change. Did she wear these clothes at home? From her expression, he had no confidence she would divulge the truth.

Offering no acknowledgement, she slid onto the bar stool next to him. He pointed at his bottle, but she shook her head. 'What's this about, Simon? There can't be anything that needs to be dealt with tonight. Whatever it is can wait until tomorrow.'

The sharp, disinterested tone irritated him. If so dismissive, why come? He wouldn't tip-toe his way through the conversation. 'Ahmed doesn't think we have enough experience in the team.'

The facial expression didn't change. Perhaps his revelation hadn't come as a surprise. 'Aaron has confidence in us.'

Something flashed beneath the surface of her serious face, but had disappeared before he identified it. Had Aaron confided business issues during their liaisons? He pushed the thought away as irrelevant and ploughed on with the negative thoughts that crowded his mind. 'That won't count when the money men want changes.'

'Aaron is desperate for success and he wants to control it.'

'No, he will sell us short if the money's right.'

Stiffening her shoulders, she pressed her lips together, disapproving of his blunt words.

He had a reaction out of her, even if minimal. A glint of irritation shone in her eyes. With a flick of her wrist, she pointed to his bottle of Bud. 'May I?'

Simon didn't want a distraction in this conversation, so he nodded and pushed the bottle along the counter. Taking a swig, she handed it back. He took a mouthful and returned it to the bar.

Lifting her chin, she eyed him with cold disinterest, 'Financiers are no good without a product.' She gave a false, derisive laugh and slapped the flat of her hand down on the counter. 'Simon, focus on the obvious. We, that's you Sadie, Dan and I own the product, it's too early for Ahmed and Aaron to claim intellectual copyright.' She spoke slowly and with emphasis, as though talking to a child. 'The only true definition of our products is in our heads.'

'But Aaron will milk us for all his worth.' A sheen of sweat covered his forehead as he raked his hands through his hair. His heart hammered and he willed himself to calm down while Evelyn stared calmly around the bar. He sucked air into his lungs and with an exasperated sigh, he blundered on, 'He's taking advantage. When he has the specifications which he's nagging us about, then it will be goodbye to the four of us and he will hand it over to Ahmed's team.' His knuckles turned white again as he gripped the bottle on the bar.

She glanced at his hand and then back at his face with scornful eyes. Her hand almost stroked his as she took the bottle from him and lifted it to her lips. Mesmerized, he waited for a response, so he nodded to the barman as he placed another bottle next to Evelyn, but she ignored it and drank from Simon's. 'I agree with you, Simon.'

The unexpected words made him pause. His body tensed. His frown deepened as his provocative mood came to the fore, 'If you agree, then we should stick together.' He challenged with a sudden note of sharpness in his voice.

'That's what we are doing.'

'No, it's damned well not.' He banged his empty bottle on the bar. His breathing became ragged. 'You're creeping behind my back to Aaron and trying to be appointed as the team leader.' The words dragged themselves from his throat. 'You want to be his technical director when the business expands.'

Unmoved by the vehemence in his voice, she offered him the new bottle. He shook his spinning head. Lucid thinking eluded him. She whispered, 'Drink.'

Without taking his eyes from her, he grabbed the bottle and gulped. The icy cold liquid flowed down his dry throat but did nothing to assuage the rising panic that welled within him.

Reaching across, she took the bottle, raised it to her lips, then wiped the back of her hand across her mouth and slid the bottle back onto the bar. Her harsh voice cut through the swirling fog in his brain, jerking him back to reality. 'You don't get on well with Aaron, it's obvious to me he will not confide in you.'

Her words cut through him. Why did she think that? He stared wildly at her, searching for an explanation. The expression gave nothing away. 'He appointed me.'

'That's a mystery to me.'

With a venomous scowl, he gritted his teeth to control his mounting anxiety. 'You think you should be team leader.' Anger laced his voice.

'That's not important now.' She wafted her hand around in a dismissive gesture. 'Our future depends on being at the centre of what's happening. Believe me, Aaron doesn't want Ahmed taking control. He appointed the four of us and will stick with his decision.'

'How do you know?'

She took another gulp of Bud. 'Believe me, Simon. I will protect you, I promise. Don't ring me in the evening again.' She slid off the bar stool in one swift movement. 'Good night.'

She picked her way through the milling crowds and disappeared. Simon had been taken by surprise by her abrupt departure. He couldn't think what to say to her, but became determined she should appreciate his point of view. By then, she had left. With a scowl, he leapt off the stool. It was time she learnt a few home truths. He stormed towards the exit and rushed into the car park. His eyes frantically scanned the area. She'd vanished.

The barman had followed him, 'You haven't paid.'

'I know.'

He handed the man a ten-pound note.

'Dumped you, has she?' The mockery in his voice made Simon cringe.

Through clenched teeth, he mumbled, 'Bitch.'

14

After a frenetic drive around the busy town circular road through the evening traffic, Simon slammed the front door of his flat. His cheeks burned with anger. Relaxation was beyond him.

Every nerve in his body jangled and because of his frustration, he'd run a red light on the way home. The journey to Norton hadn't been long, but his driving had been poor. The fury with Evelyn hadn't dissipated as the action plan with her had backfired, but he knew where he stood. She would stitch him up at any opportunity. Trust her? No chance.

His eyes scanned the clean and tidy flat. The evening hadn't panned out as he'd expected. Candice had rejected him and Evelyn wanted his job. Two attractive females who didn't care about him. Determination gripped him, as he needed to focus and devise a plan to deal with those who wished to undermine him. Nodding his head in approval at his own thoughts, he made coffee and took it to the small back room in his flat where he kept his home computer.

'Hello, Simon.' The tinny voice of Dess echoed around the small room. He stared with distrust at the black speaker as he needed to be wary of Dess. Sadie had been collecting the data from people's computers. She had promised to delete the conversations and only to record the emotional analysis, but Simon wouldn't trust her or anyone else.

'Hi, Dess.' Simon forced a false joviality, 'I've had a good day but I'm going to rebuild the computer.'

'Okay. Anything I can help with?'

'No, thanks.'

Settling in front of the computer, he prepared himself for a long session. With a tight-lipped smile, Simon found the Dess program and deleted it. As part of the team, he'd installed Dan's controls, but not in his sacrosanct computer room, he wouldn't be snooped on. They only monitored the lounge and kitchen.

Now for the serious business, he squared his shoulders

as though preparing for a fight. Aaron wanted to replace him with Evelyn. After her reaction tonight, he knew where he stood. His mind worked and clarity gradually came. Before he acted, he would search for crucial information.

He logged on to the office computers and found the place where he'd set up the email accounts for everyone in the office. They used emails extensively so there would be interesting material there. As a personal insurance, when he set up the accounts, he made sure he kept a copy of everyone's password before encryption. Serious times called for serious measures, he'd never had to use the information before, but his job was under threat.

He would start with Evelyn, so he logged onto the system as her. He breathed a sigh of relief as the password he'd stored worked. Evelyn's emails came onto his screen. He read carefully through them. Despite the stress, he smiled. Dan had been trying it on with her. He'd made many attempts to arrange a meeting out of work. Evelyn hadn't responded. Checking the dates, he gathered Dan had given up trying.

Here's one of interest. It's a reply from Aaron. An email had asked Aaron why she hadn't been appointed team leader. Aaron had replied he had other ideas for her when the company expanded. He hinted he would require a Technical Director and she would be well placed. The end of the email caught Simon's attention. 'Why don't we meet outside of work to talk about the future. Same place as before.'

A reply from Evelyn to Sadie caught Simon's attention. She did not know of the bracelet and despite Sadie's accusations, it had not been under the desk that morning. Simon had also searched for it. In a broad and not subtle hint, Sadie thought Evelyn had taken it, although she flatly denied the accusation.

Let me search Aaron's emails. They are likely to be the most revealing. This job will take all night. There are so many. Simon picked the ones addressed to Ahmed. He sipped his coffee as he studied them. As he suspected, Ahmed doesn't consider that he is competent. He has a far more experienced friend searching for a job. Simon trawled the emails until tiredness overcame him. As he prepared for bed, his mind was full of wild plans about how to deal with Evelyn and Ahmed. Did he have any allies? The women he ruled out. Dan? He would fight for his job as a weak link in the business. Perhaps it would be time to have a quiet out of work drink with him?

15

Dan believed his resolution to work hard had paid dividends but there was still a mountain to climb for his work to be acceptable. Why had he been texted on his way to work about an emergency meeting? It had never happened before. Not being an early starter, he would be late and the last to arrive. The flexi time suited him as he found early mornings a strain and preferred to work into the evening when the office was quiet.

With the outer area empty, he made his way to Aaron's office. A feeling of tension greeted him the minute he entered the room. Aaron and his three colleagues sat at the table. The warmth of the room made him slip off his fleece. He slumped down on the remaining seat with the watery sunshine on his back. Normally he would have made a joke about arriving late, but stony faces greeted him. Grunting a good morning, he searched faces to discover the purpose of the meeting.

Aaron's pale face creased with a worried frown as he fiddled with a pen that lay on top of his daybook. Perhaps his pallid complexion resulted from the pressure of the business. Dan couldn't be worried about Aaron as he struggled with his own work. The subdued expressions and silence from the others gave him no hint. Hopefully, the meeting would end quickly so he could focus on his project. He'd be surprised if he left tonight before ten o'clock as he had so much to do.

Aaron drew in a deep breath. 'I won't beat about the bush. Initially, I had been informed by Evelyn that her system had been compromised last night. But now Sadie has said that someone has been reading her emails. We do not know the extent of this incursion, Evelyn, can you update us on what you found.'

'As I've had my computer hacked before, I've installed code to detect activity on my account. Last night someone read my emails.'

Dan peered around the group, unsure of what else everyone knew. There must have been a discussion before he'd arrived. 'Any clues?' He examined their faces.

Evelyn shook her head. 'No, my monitoring system showed it was me, but I never logged on. There were no other clues.'

Sadie and Simon had grim, worried faces. Sadie shuffled in her chair. 'I have a similar monitor to Evelyn, so someone has been on my computer without my agreement. My emails were read but I can't find evidence the intruder checked anything else.'

Aaron stared at the group. 'What about you, Simon?'

'I've no checker on mine. So, if someone examined my emails and didn't make changes, then I wouldn't know.'

Dan kept his eyes on those around the table. This situation could become serious. 'I'm the same as Simon. I've no device so I don't know whether anyone has read them.' Tension gripped him as he thought through his email trail. There was nothing incriminating in his emails he could recall, but those he'd originally sent to Evelyn could be embarrassing as he'd wanted to meet her after work, but she had never replied.

For some unknown reason, he'd kept the emails he had sent or drafted and had never deleted them. They were of no interest to anyone else, but he resolved to erase them at the first available opportunity. As others shuffled in their seats, he was bold. 'What about you, Aaron?'

Aaron jerked his head up from the papers he had been shuffling. 'Same as you. I don't have an email monitoring program.' His forehead creased with concern. 'Perhaps I'd better install one.'

Silence hung over the group. No one made eye contact. Dan remained silent as a multitude of questions swirled. A chill ran through him, despite sweating in the hot sun on his back. He'd worked from home yesterday evening. This could be difficult if he didn't handle it well. Would they immediately think him guilty of breaking into the system? Anxiety gripped him. His gaze darted around the assembled group. 'Aaron, I worked on the systems late last night.'

'In the office?'

'No, over a remote connection from home, I tidied up

a server but not the one which has the email accounts and I installed system and security updates on each machine.'

Aaron stared hard at him, 'Show us.'

Had he been accused? Four unsmiling faces watched his every move. With a sweaty hand, he pulled the keyboard on the table towards him.

Aaron picked up the remote and clicked a button. A screen descended from the ceiling against the end wall of the office. Dan flicked at the keyboard and the ceiling projector came into life. He logged on. Everyone watched his keystrokes.

The lengthening silence in the room unnerved him, but he moved the cursor to the operating system for the server farm of computers. 'What do you want to view first?' He glanced across at Aaron.

'The server you worked on.'

'It's a sandpit for testing our ideas. We agreed it needed categorising so we could find our various attempts. Last night I moved the files to under people's names.' A nervous tension arose in his dry throat. 'A simple job that I'd been promising to complete.'

Aaron leaned forward. 'Are you sure you didn't go on to the email server?'

Conscious that all eyes in the room stared at him, he gulped, and his forehead beaded with sweat. A frisson of guilt swept through him, although he was innocent as he hadn't accessed the email server.

'Positive. I did nothing to the email server.' He forced a smile. He tapped at the keyboard again. The root directory of the email server came up. 'I'll load the log file of the email server activity. That should tell us about unusual access.'

A note of firmness crept into his voice. This breach of security had nothing to do with him, but with his expertise, he might be able to track down the problem. With these thoughts in mind, his tension eased. Knowing they required his expertise gave him a sense of importance.

The dates popped up on the screen. Aaron sighed. 'No one has changed anything for weeks. There is the list of people accessing their own emails. Simon, you were on last night, also you Dan and the two accesses on Evelyn's and Sadie's account, which they say isn't them.'

'There were admin changes last month.' Dan pointed towards the screen.

'I added a couple of guest accounts,' snapped Simon.

'We're getting nowhere.' Aaron leaned back and ran his fingers through his hair.

Evelyn tapped her fingernails on the table. Her impatience with the situation became obvious. With a frozen smile, 'Aaron. This is important.' Her tone brooked no negotiation. 'Someone has been spying on me and I expect it to be sorted.'

Dan couldn't be sure, but did she glance at Simon.

'I agree,' Sadie interjected, without taking her eyes from Evelyn.

A hush descended on the room. The only sound was the low hum of the computer.

Simon broke the uneasy silence. 'Do you want me to investigate further?'

'No, I need you and Evelyn with me to agree on a way forward for our triangle of products.'

Aaron's eyes swept across Sadie and came to rest on Dan. 'You know your way around the servers and systems in this office, don't you?' Dan acknowledged with a slight dip of his head.

'I want a thorough investigation. How did someone read Evelyn's emails without her permission?' Before Sadie could speak, Aaron added, 'And check out Sadie's. It's time-consuming for you, Dan, but needs to be done.' A flash of irritation glinted in his narrowed eyes. 'Can you report back later this afternoon?'

Dan nodded. Although he was busy and needed to spend time on his project, a sense of importance filled him that Aaron had singled him out for the task. Aaron pushed back his chair and rose to his feet, signalling the end of the meeting. 'Now let's get some work done.'

16

Dan enjoyed a challenge and had considered a career in computer forensics. Having cleared his computer of his current work, it would be time to find the hacker. He would enjoy his investigation.

The office worked in silence for an hour as tension pervaded the air. Evelyn and Simon had only a short meeting with Aaron before returning to their desks without speaking. The tapping of keyboards, rustling papers and the odd loud sigh were the only sounds to be heard. No one moved from their desk. Even Sadie made no quips or comments. The thick silence stretched and hung in the air.

Dan fidgeted. How long would this atmosphere last? Rolling the stress from his shoulders, he ploughed on with his research. A slow methodical approach involving checking and rechecking the data. The sound that broke the silence and distracted him came from the rattle of the exterior door.

Aaron returned with no discernible improvement on his morose face. He slipped his mobile into his pocket as he entered the office. Why go outside to make a call? With a sharp voice, Aaron called Evelyn and Simon to join him.

As soon as the office door shut, Sadie edged around the desks to him. A strange approach, as she normally stayed at her seat and called out. In a quiet voice, not typical of her, 'Let's catch an early lunch. I didn't have any breakfast.'

Torn between the investigation and chatting with Sadie, his memory flicked back to the meal at the Manor. They had laughed and gossiped about their lives, telling each other amusing anecdotes and the evening had slipped by. He'd accompanied her home after they had eaten and put the world to rights, but he didn't fish for an invitation for coffee but thought that he might progress with her if he remained patient.

With reluctance, he shook his head, 'I will work through.'

Resting her hand on his arm, she whispered, 'Come on, Dan. I need to speak to you.' She winked at him, 'It's about what you're doing.'

His eyes opened wide as he stood up. Did she have information that might help? She had insisted in the meeting that her email had been compromised. 'Lead on.'

Within minutes, they had grabbed a table at the nearby McDonald's. The bright basic interior held indifference for him, but he used it as a place to eat when hungry. Patting his stomach, he ordered, a Big Mac with extra fries. When he had settled into his job, he would deal with his unhealthy diet of convenience food. Sadie chose veggie dippers with a side salad.

The main seating area was not busy, although there was a long queue for the drive through. Sadie led the way to a corner table with no one nearby.

'I'm not staying long as I want to solve the email issue. What did you want to say?'

She chewed thoughtfully on a dipper. 'Evelyn has caused the problem.'

'What!' Dan stared in open mouthed astonishment. 'She's the one who reported it to Aaron.'

She ignored his reaction. 'Of course, she would. She had been going through my emails but spotted I had a tracker on, so she invented the story to cover herself.'

Rocking back in his seat, he stared out of the window at the heavily articulated lorries trundling to the motorway. Sadie's wild idea confused him. He gave an exasperated laugh. 'This is ridiculous. What is her motive?'

Sadie leaned forward in a conspiratorial manner, glancing around to make sure there was no one in the vicinity. 'I've not told you before, Dan, but I can trust you.' He became wary of the conversation. 'She stole my bracelet.' A cynical smile twisted her lips. Dan shook his head. Sadie had been more fun with a couple of glasses of wine inside her. She had a bee in her bonnet about Evelyn and the damned missing bracelet.

Taking a long glug of his coke to control his irritability. 'Even I can spot the signs with Evelyn.'

'What signs?'

'She's rich, her clothes are high class. I checked the label on her jacket and looked it up. Several hundred quid. The bracelet is sentimental for you and not worth much. Why would she want to steal it?'

'I don't know.' Sadie pouted her lips. 'That's the problem. My theory is that Evelyn must have hidden it in her desk and then it fell on the floor. If she had given it back to me, then I wouldn't have taken any notice.'

Sadie wouldn't drop the disappearance of the bracelet. Her obsession appeared unnecessary and irritated him. He'd have one more go at trying to give a reasonable explanation. 'You could have been mistaken.' His strained voice had an edge of irritation. 'Perhaps a cable connector glistened in the light.'

'I knew you wouldn't believe me.' Sadie flopped back in her seat and folded her arms across her chest, 'I shouldn't have told you.' The petulant sounding voice grated on Dan.

Wiping his hand across his face, 'I'm a simple type of guy and don't go for conspiracy theory.'

She stood up with scorn written on her face and narrowed her eyes. 'Bear in mind what I've said as you do your checking.' Grabbing the remains of her salad, she stomped away, leaving him to eat the rest of his lunch on his own.

He didn't rush to finish and chewed thoughtfully, enjoying the peace and solitude. He mulled over the problems that faced him. Someone had snooped the email accounts. Although only Evelyn and Sadie could be certain, he didn't doubt that the other email accounts would have been opened. He had assumed that he should search for an external hacker, but could it be someone from inside?

Nothing convinced him either way, but he would keep an open mind. It presented itself as another avenue to explore, so his thoughts switched to Aaron. His mood this morning had been grumpy, with his irritation obvious. Had the email problem upset him or had something else happened?

This time Aaron had asked him to investigate, but with another security breach, would Aaron employ external people? He nodded to himself, convinced that would happen so he would need to delete some material he had on his computers, especially the emails relating to Evelyn and the pictures he had taken of her using the security cameras. They could easily be interpreted as harassment. The office atmosphere, which had appeared so stable when they started together, had become vindictive.

He squared his shoulders as he would be squeaky clean. His secret place on the servers would have to be deleted, as an expert would discover the incriminating information. He'd delete everything. When he returned to the office, he would work in the server room.

Two hours after lunch, he opened the door back into the brightness and warmth of the main office. He had finished. A sense of satisfaction swept through him, but it soon vanished as his news would shock Aaron. He knocked and opened Aaron's office door. To his surprise, Ahmed and Candice were there, so he mumbled an apology.

'Any news on the emails?' Aaron beckoned him to enter the office. He nodded. 'I haven't explained to Candice and Ahmed what you are doing, but they need to know. Sit down, Dan, and tell us what you've discovered.'

Settling himself, he stared at the three solemn faces, who peered at him expectantly. He would choose his words carefully, to ensure they understood the implications of his findings.

Disbelief had flooded through him when he'd formulated the results. With a deep breath and a neutral and business-like voice, 'To recap, Evelyn and Sadie claimed that an unauthorised person checked their emails last night.'

Aaron flapped an impatient hand. 'What did you find out? Keep it brief.'

He suspected that Aaron had lost interest. He hadn't been sympathetic to their complaints this morning and his manner had been bordering on dismissive. 'Evelyn and Sadie had monitoring software. No one else does.'

'What does that mean?' Candice placed her phone down on the table and gave him her full attention. 'I can't tell whether only those two accounts were compromised or all of them.'

Ahmed's icy and accusing voice cut in, 'Have you been

reading our emails?'

He shook his head. Neither Ahmed nor Candice understood the mysteries of computer hardware. 'I'm responsible for the server. The emails are encrypted so I can't read them. They can only be read if the snooper has the password.'

'I never give my password to anyone,' snapped Ahmed.

He ignored Ahmed's aggression. 'Neither would Evelyn nor Sadie.'

Aaron asked, 'Has the password file been breached?'

'No one has changed their password for at least a week and the password file is undisturbed since then.'

Ahmed shrugged. 'Evelyn and Sadie must have inadvertently given their passwords away.'

Aaron wrinkled his brow, 'How many email accounts are there?'

'Four in the outer office, two guest accounts that have never been used and you three.'

Aaron raised his eyebrows. 'I didn't realise you had an account, Candice or you Ahmed.'

Candice shrugged, 'Not long after we started, Simon explained he had set up an email account for me.'

'Same with me.' Ahmed flicked a dismissive hand.

Candice retrieved her phone and, with head lowered, flicked at the keypad.

'For goodness' sake, Candice. Leave that! You need to concentrate. Dan's investigation is important.'

'Are the email accounts secure?' Ahmed's brow creased with worry.

Dan shook his head, 'Some unusual activity took place on the email server last night.'

Aaron focused on him, 'What type of activity?'

'Someone deleted a file.'

'Is that significant?' Candice struggled to concentrate on the conversation and kept flicking her eyes at the wall clock.

Dan sensed Aaron had guessed the implication so he focused on him, 'It could have been a rogue file that trapped passwords but didn't encrypt them. The hacker could gain access to the email accounts.'

'So we don't know whether someone has read my emails?' Candice fidgeted with her phone again.

Ahmed returned his full concentration to the discussion. 'Would they have time? Isn't it likely to be someone interested in one person?'

'No.' Aaron's eyes narrowed. 'Once someone gained access, they could download them and read them later. Ahmed, forget about personal issues; this could be industrial espionage.' A look of alarm flashed across his face, but he made no comment. 'Could you track how they accessed our systems, Dan?' Aaron drummed his fingers on the table as he fixed him with a hard stare.

Dan wriggled in his seat and an uncertain smile twitched at his lips. He paused as he struggled to find the right words. 'I tried, but you won't be pleased with the implications. I checked the login server and the firewalls and all seven accounts were logged on.'

'I went out. I didn't send any emails.' Candice blurted. 'Does that mean someone used my computer?'

Aaron smiled indulgently at his wife. 'I expect you ticked a box to say keep you permanently logged in. We probably all have.' All eyes swivelled back to Dan. They waited with grim faces to hear his explanation.

'No activity was apparent on the external logs and no files transfer was detected through the firewall.'

'What's that mean?' interrupted Ahmed.

'One of the seven of us checked those emails.' With a dead-pan face, 'Over to you, Aaron. The system only proves it is one of the seven, so we are all in the frame unless you have another way of discovering the culprit.'

17

Dan sat in the chilly server room having struggled through the early morning gloom. Despite a few beers on the previous evening with his mates, he'd struggled to sleep. The worry of keeping his job had swirled in his tormented mind, as his accumulated debts would not be cleared quickly.

Desperate to keep his job, he arrived in the server room armed with a cup of strong coffee on a cold, wet Saturday morning before seven o'clock. The arrangement had been to meet at ten o'clock, so that allowed him three hours to further investigate the servers.

The muscles along his jawline clenched with determination. He planned to find the culprit for the email hacks even though Aaron had lost interest. He wanted to pursue the matter for his own personal satisfaction and discover the person who had been devious. Dealing with it in his own way seemed the best approach. He hadn't mentioned it to the others, including Aaron, but had set parameters on the servers to seek unusual activity. Next time a problem occurred, he would be ahead of everyone else.

He wanted to be valuable to the business. With a quiver of guilt, he flicked at the computer that controlled the security settings for the office. Aaron had wanted an in-house system, so he had asked Dan to install and monitor it during his first days with the business. The cameras were supposed to operate only in an empty office, but without permission, he had set them to record continuously.

This move might pick up information that would pinpoint the culprit. He opened the log on the screen, which showed unexpected activity in the main office late last night. He located the reference and turned on the recording.

The camera in the main office had picked up Sadie as she prowled the office. His mind had raced searching for answers as she'd left work at the same time as him, early evening. Had she forgotten something and returned? Whatever the reason, it must be important to lure her back so late. He made himself comfortable to watch the excerpt through to the conclusion.

Sadie moved cautiously and her head swivelled from side to side as though checking for someone else's presence. In her arms she clutched a large dark shape. His attention became captivated, and a furrow of confusion wrinkled his brow. Sadie trod with slow precision past her own desk to Evelyn's. Pausing, she unfurled the shape she carried, a blanket. A frown of puzzlement flashed across his face. What was she doing?

With outstretched arms holding the blanket, she threw it over the screen. He smiled at Sadie's apprehension and her dislike of Evelyn's avatar. But it didn't explain her presence in the office at Evelyn's desk.

Sadie had a key to the building and so would have expected the cameras to be disabled by her legal means of entry. Sadie opened the drawers of Evelyn's desk and rummaged through them while still wearing her cycling gloves. She must be searching for the bracelet, which she still believed Evelyn had stolen. Sadie shook her head and slid the drawer closed. With pinched lips, her eyes scanned the desk. Dropping to her knees, she then disappeared under the desk.

Sadie wouldn't let the missing bracelet rest, but her intensity would destroy what was left of the harmonious relationship in the office. But she would lose out as Evelyn had become popular with Aaron. Sadie eventually stopped her search, retrieved the blanket and left the office. Dan waited until the office lights went out.

18

Aaron pulled on a thick jumper and searched for his wallet in the dimly lit bedroom. Shivering at the throbbing pulse of rain beating against the window, he perched on the edge of the bed and flicked at his phone and searched for the app. 'Dess.'

'Good morning, Aaron.' The usual chirpy reply. 'How can I help you?'

'Take the car from the garage and enable the climate control.'

'Yes, Aaron.' Silence filled the bedroom. Movement made him peer towards the wriggling mound of the duvet. Candice rolled over in the bed and her bleary eyes searched his face.

'Aaron, it's seven o'clock on a Saturday morning. It's slinging it down; you can't be playing golf, so why not come back to bed?'

'Go back to sleep, Candice, I'm going into work as the others will be there and it's important that we make progress.' Candice groaned and dragged the duvet over her head. 'If you took more interest, you'd realise time is crucial.' He gazed with irritation at the wriggling form under the bedclothes. 'Why don't you come and help?'

The duvet shot back, 'Don't be so bloody stupid, I can't help. I'm not technical.'

He scowled, 'I realise that only too well my darling, but how about using your domestic skills to organise coffee and fetch the workers some lunch?'

'Piss off.' The mound reformed under the duvet.

'Pathetic,' muttered Aaron as he tied his trainers. He sprung up from the bed, causing it to jolt, which brought another groan from Candice. He slammed the bedroom door as he left and a small smile of rebellion crossed his face. The cold, wet morning greeted him as he jogged briskly towards the waiting Ziani. The security lights lit up the car where droplets of water gleamed on its highly polished grey surface.

The car had navigated from the garage to a point near the front door, and the interior had been warmed in readiness for his arrival. Flicking the navigate button on the central screen, he pressed Office. Its external sensors continually worked and responded accordingly. As the car drove him to work, he listened to his emails. At least there had been no repetition of the email snooping after the first incident, which occurred over a week ago.

Dan, Sadie and Simon had agreed to work on Saturday and would start about ten o'clock. Evelyn had texted Aaron, informing him she would be in the office by seven thirty. A slow smile came to his lips and his breath quickened. The memory of their last pleasurable evening together flooded his mind. The anticipation of meeting Evelyn alone had motivated him to jump out of bed early this morning.

The Ziani pulled up in front of the office block. As he got out, he tapped his phone to open the app and instructed the car to park itself, then strolled through the entrance foyer and unlocked the office. He'd only flicked on the computer in his office when he heard the outside door. Glancing up, he grinned at Evelyn as she came into his office and dropped her heavy coat in the nearest chair. He moved behind the desk but remained standing and held out his arms. Her cheeks flushed as she wrapped her arms around him, kissing him with a passion that took his breath away. With a relaxed movement, she pressed her body against him.

She would be too much of a distraction. He needed to focus on the business. Swallowing hard, he ignored the sensations which swirled through his body. With reluctance, he broke away and crumpled into his chair. She positioned herself in the chair by his desk and raised her eyes, while a sultry smile edged its way across her lips. 'Can we meet next week?'

'Yes, Candice is in London on Wednesday, so I'll try to persuade her to stay over.' He focused intently on her face.

'Good, we won't have to watch the clock and can spend the whole night together.'

Aaron rubbed his hand over his face and attempted to push away the images of her shapely, naked body. With a roll of his shoulders and a silent sigh, he opened the folder on his desk. 'What progress on the integration?'

'Good, although the others resisted at first.'

'I didn't know about any problems.' He jerked his head up. 'Why didn't you come and tell me.'

'It would have made the matter worse. The other three are suspicious of the number of times we talk.'

Aaron drummed his fingers on the desk. 'None of them know about our meeting outside of work, do they?'

'No, we've been discreet.'

Aaron paused as his mind whirled through the implications of his affair with Evelyn. Did anyone suspect? He had been careful with his approach to her in the office. His confidence returned. No one knew, so he focused on the current problem. 'What resistance have you had? And who from? I want to know.'

'Perhaps I've been strong in my words, but I suggested what I wanted from them for integrating their systems, but they disagreed.' With an intense expression on her face, 'Simon had planned how it should be implemented and the others agreed with him. They never involved me in their discussions but endeavoured to suggest it to me as a solution.'

Aaron shuffled in his seat. It would be hard enough to finish the software without the team arguing about the best way to join it together. 'What's the difference between their approach and yours?'

'They want me to write the code to join each separate part of their modules together.'

'Okay.' Aaron opened his daybook and scribbled notes. 'That seems a standard approach in the IT industry, so why do you want to do it differently?'

'I checked through their work. Simon's isn't bad, but Dan and Sadie have weak code which might cause us problems, so I told them I wanted entire access to their code.'

Aaron doubted her approach, but he'd appointed Evelyn to integrate the triangle of software and he needed to back her, otherwise the whole business would fall apart. 'Is the resistance resolved?'

'Yes, in principle. If they didn't agree to my method, then we would come and meet you.'

'Did that settle it?'

'Yes, but it hasn't made for a relaxed atmosphere in the outer office as it's three against me. They would like me to fail.'

He had examined the modules. Sadie had good ideas, but she lacked programming expertise. Dan had been slapdash in his code and that might lead to hidden errors. Simon, systematic but slow and pedantic, had produced good work. He had to back Evelyn as no other workable option presented itself.

'They ought to be thankful they still have a job.'

'Why?'

'After the scare about reading emails, Ahmed threatened to withdraw his backing for the project.'

Evelyn's stern face never changed, although her eyes flashed, 'Has he something to hide?'

A strange remark! He studied her closely, but then shrugged. 'I don't know, but the email episode upset him. When can we demonstrate a prototype? All that he has glimpsed so far is Dess.'

'Soon, provided the others help.'

'They will!'

A small smile twisted her lips. 'Dess will be withdrawn this morning. I will return it to operation when fully integrated.'

He stood and moved to the back of Evelyn's chair and rested his hand on the nape of her neck. She didn't look around or respond to the touch.

'It's not sensible, Aaron. Not in the office as we need to keep it professional, so we have a united face towards the others. When Ahmed witnesses the success of the finished triangle of products, it will be less stressful.'

'Maybe.'

Evelyn's sudden head movement made him jump. 'That camera in the corner flashed.'

He stared at it as he moved away from her. 'It often does, it's only active when the burglar alarm is set. The red flash is the motion detector, it's not spying on us.'

She strutted towards the door. 'It makes me nervous.' As she reached the door, she stopped. 'I still want to know who read my emails.'

He had become fed up with the trivial email problem being raised again. 'Forget about it. Get on with your work.'

Curling her top lip, she left the office, shutting the door with a thud.

19

Dan blew out a long breath as he pulled his jacket tight in the chilly server room. Sadie's behaviour would result in the sack. She resisted advice. He would focus on his own problems. Time to finish with the servers and concentrate on his project. He had a quick flick through the footage from the outside cameras. Nothing of interest so he examined the recording logs. One had recorded this morning, only a few minutes ago. His eyes widened and he hovered the cursor over the playback button. Who had arrived in the office?

A tentative smile etched its way across his face. No one would realise he had arrived as he'd kept his coat on because of the usual chill in the server room. He'd also re-locked the front door after arriving. Flicking the playback button Aaron sat in his office. As his finger hovered over the stop button, Evelyn appeared. She wrapped her arms around Aaron's neck and they kissed. Long and slow. Transfixed by the scene which unfolded, his breath stalled. A wide smile covered his face. So, the rumour was true. Aaron massaged Evelyn's neck and kissed her again.

Watching until Evelyn left the office, he picked her up again on the main office camera. She had no smile and her face was impassive as she strode towards her desk. No one would have guessed what had happened in Aaron's office from her reactions a few seconds later.

An idea popped into his mind. Evelyn had become the key person in the business, so perhaps he should transfer his allegiance to her. He'd not succeeded in persuading her to meet outside work so he would strive for a professional relationship.

Keeping an eye on the cameras, he waited until the main office cleared. Evelyn had moved to the kitchen to make coffee. Aaron sat at the desk in his office. Dan sneaked out of the server room, closed the door quietly and nipped across to the main door which he let go with a swish and called out, 'Morning all, it's nippy out there.' Opening the corner cupboard, he hung up his large jacket.

Evelyn emerged with a fixed glare from the kitchen area and mumbled, 'Good morning.' She sat at her desk but took no notice of Dan's movement towards the kitchen. He made his coffee and planned his approach.

'Evelyn,' she glanced up with a flicker of irritation in her eyes but didn't reply. 'It's not urgent but when you have some time, I'd appreciate a chat about how you perceive integrating my work.' It sounded bland, but he ploughed on regardless, 'In that way I might be able to tweak my programming to fit your integration.'

Almost a smile, 'Now?'

He nodded at the unexpected answer. For reasons he was unable to explain, nervousness gripped him as he drew a chair up next to her and pasted a smile on his tense face. Perhaps one of his tasks had been completed as it was the first time, he had received any encouragement from her, but his next involvement with Aaron would be critical and even though days away his stomach twisted into a knot.

20

Dan slipped into the passenger seat of the Ziani, 'Good morning, Aaron.' Aaron clicked the navigate button on the large centre screen and typed in Hopwood Services but switched off the satnav sound.

'Are we meeting him at the motorway services?'

'Yes, he's busy, so it's difficult to arrange, but he's the main technical man in Ahmed's consortium and wants to meet his opposite number in the team, which is you.'

Dan pushed his chest out with pride. Perhaps his career with TechMatt might go somewhere. 'But why the Services?'

'He's staying in Birmingham but flying home after our meeting.'

Dan was more interested in the car as Aaron drove rapidly through the lanes south of Sheffield towards the M1. 'Where's home?'

'Nigeria.'

'Have you met him before?'

'No, he's a friend of Ahmed.'

He became wary, 'You'll be leading the meeting, won't you?'

'Relax, Dan, the meeting will be fine. Be honest and open about the technical issues.'

'Is he technical?'

'Ahmed assures me he has a PhD in computing from Massachusetts Institute of Technology.'

Dan lapsed into silence as his stomach clenched itself into a tight, uncomfortable knot as he had never been confident in his own abilities and being questioned by someone on top of his game appeared a daunting and scary prospect. He remained lost in a wave of negative thoughts about his ability to deal with the situation as Aaron took a couple of calls. Would today make or break him? He would try his best but suspected it wouldn't be good enough, although he hoped Aaron might give him a decent reference.

Aaron accelerated hard down the slip road, throwing

Dan back in his seat. Aaron flicked at the stalk. 'There, it'll take us along the motorway on autopilot.' He lazily left his hand on the steering wheel, 'Now I've you on your own, how's the atmosphere in the office.'

'Anything in particular?'

Aaron gave him a frosty glance. 'Sadie and Evelyn don't get on. Is it still about that damned bracelet?'

'Yep, it makes meetings difficult, but I've told Sadie to forget about it, but she niggles at any opportunity.'

'That's the right approach. Have you tried with Evelyn?'

'I would, but she hardly talks to me and only if it's about work. She's a mystery and appears to have a jumbo sign saying keep away.'

Aaron grimaced. 'How is Simon progressing?'

He wondered whether there was a catch or trick in the question, but nothing registered on Aaron's face. 'We have struck up an accord, but he's always too stressed out for his own good.'

'Should I replace him as team leader?'

'No, definitely not. Simon's a good man and deserves his position, he's tolerant and calm with Evelyn, which is more than Sadie, or I would be.'

Dan leaned back in the low armchair and sweated as he sipped his second cup of coffee from Starbucks. The upstairs area of the services swarmed with people. Aaron, Emmanuel and Dan had squeezed into a corner table at the end of the café.

The questioning from Emmanuel had been gruelling as he pounced on any hesitation and then a raft of further questions followed. Dan liked him as a character but couldn't be sure how much to trust him in an on-the-fly meeting in the motorway services. If Aaron hadn't been there, he wouldn't have told Emmanuel anything.

The large Nigerian leaned back in his chair and took a deep breath. 'I've a crucial question and it's the most difficult.'

Dan inwardly groaned, were the questions never going to end? Straightening his back, he drew his lips into a thin line and concentrated on Emmanuel, who fixed him with his large brown eyes.

'The initial idea is okay. Not brilliant, but okay. What I'm concerned about is the follow-up. What will make us money? Tell me what you will do next after you've connected various objects together.

Dan's stomach lurched as he had struggled with the first ideas and had never discussed with Aaron what would come next. With Sadie and Simon, he had aired some idle thoughts as they played table tennis one evening. A sudden deep frown creased Aaron's forehead. Raising his eyebrows, Dan tried to gauge whether to speak or to let Aaron deal with the question.

Aaron took a deep breath. 'Go on, Dan.'

With no option, he had to give his opinion. 'Can I take the example of the Ziani?'

'Yes. This sounds intriguing.' Emmanuel leaned forward to give Dan his full concentration.

'The satnav has the details of a journey, and my app will anticipate homecoming and communicate with objects at home to set them accordingly. It will prompt for the slow cooker to be switched on, whether to order a takeaway or turn up the heating.'

'The driver might have overload and reject the system.'

He had to dig deep for his answer, but it had been reading Evelyn's proposal that had suggested the solution. 'Heating and security can be set from recognising patterns in behaviour. The same pattern matching can prompt questions.'

'The mobile phone and car apps exchange information. The phone app deduces that on the last three occasions the driver had arrived home late, he had visited a local pub as he had booked a table, so the app would prompt with the question to book a table, yes or no.'

Emmanuel smiled, 'Well done, Aaron. You've employed a talented man with vision, and I shall tell Ahmed that your business has my full support for expansion.'

Dan breathed a sigh of relief and slumped back in his chair. Would he be able to deliver? He waited as Aaron escorted Emmanuel to his car. Breathing a sigh of relief. His technical capabilities still concerned him, but he had made progress.

21

Sadie had given up guessing why Aaron had suddenly asked her to come with him.

He led her into the empty office space. 'What do you think, Sadie?'

'Impressive. It's large.'

The emptiness of the bright second-floor office space made her voice echo, although her heels made no sound on the carpet tiles in the wide expanse as she wandered the room. Pausing at the window, she gazed across the low-level office blocks towards the woods.

The journey time to the new office would be trivial and she could walk the route in twenty minutes. Perfect. Sadie shaded her eyes from the glare of the low sun, which shone through the full glass windows down one side of the space.

'There's room for about twenty desks.' Aaron waved an explanatory arm to show the amount of space.

The number twenty lodged in her mind. It seemed huge after working in a team of four for several months. 'Will we have that number of staff?'

'Yes, that's the plan.'

Aaron crossed the room, pushed open a door in the far corner and flicked on the light to illuminate the windowless space. She followed. 'This will be the computer room. The extra space is vital to accommodate the increased number of servers we will require as the business expands.'

Larger than the existing one but a different shape, four metres long but only a metre and a half wide. Down the long wall, a large bench stretched the full length. Aaron strolled to the end. The click of the door closing made Sadie jump. The single fluorescent light made it dark compared to the main office.

Relaxing her shoulders, she studied Aaron as he perused the space. 'This should suit Dan's requirements for a computer room.' A smile lit up his handsome face as he peered at the electrical and data sockets. 'There are plenty of data connections and power.'

She nodded, but her knowledge didn't extend to setting up computer rooms. The information didn't help, so her mind drifted back to Aaron's casual sign that there would be twenty desks. She couldn't resist any longer, 'You said that the business will expand with new staff.'

As he turned his attention from the power sockets to Sadie, she noticed how close they were in the enclosed space with only a weak light. Taller than her, he peered down to her face and his eyes flashed. 'Yes, the consortium wants me to expand rapidly with new premises and new staff.'

'What happens to us?' She gave a nervous giggle. 'Especially me. I'm not a computer whizz like the others.'

He moved closer, 'Stop fretting Sadie, we'll have enough technical people around. It's your idea that caught everyone's attention.'

A shudder passed through her, but she resolved to tell him the truth. 'But it's not going well.'

He placed his arm around her shoulder and gave it a gentle squeeze. Sadie tensed. Should her boss be acting in this manner? She shouldn't have stayed in here with him, as it would have been better to discuss the problems with her project in his office.

'There will always be glitches, we'll work it through together.' He released his grip on her shoulder and gave a soft, throaty laugh. 'Perhaps we ought to meet more often, then I can help you personally.'

An icy tremor crept up her back. Colour rushed to her cheeks and her mind whirled as she tried to fathom out the true meaning behind his ambiguous words. Dan had been convinced he was having an affair with Evelyn. Perhaps he's finished with her and is searching for someone else. Aaron's phone rang.

'I'll leave you to answer it.' With a sense of relief, she spun on her heels and left the enclosed room.

Dan had helped her so at least in the short term her technical issues would be solved, although what would happen when new staff arrived would be a different matter.

Within minutes, Sadie sat in the passenger seat of the Ziani watching the large screen used for the controls and settings of the car. Neither of them spoke. After the conversation in the cupboard, she had reached no conclusion. If he made a pass at her, it would make her life more difficult, but would it be foolish to turn him down? He was the boss.

Being in favour with him could have a great impact on her job security. If she rejected him, he might find an excuse to sack her. She shuddered as she enjoyed her job. He was handsome and exuded charm, so a sexual interlude with him might be fun.

Aaron reached the motorway and flicked on the autopilot. He'd set it for seventy miles per hour in the heavy traffic and they cruised along the middle lane, which suddenly became clear, and the Ziani accelerated away.

She gripped her seat belt. As a nervous car passenger, she became jittery when the car drove itself. After a quiet session of concentrated deep breathing as the car progressed, they left the motorway and drifted slowly into their current office park. The car parked itself in a convenient space. Being a passenger in the Ziani had sparked an idea, but she couldn't decide whether to speak but was brave. 'May I suggest an idea?'

Aaron relaxed back in the driver's seat and grinned, his teeth flashing white against his tanned face. 'I need to be inside for a call in ten minutes, but until then you've my full attention.'

'This car is almost completely self-driving.'

'Yes, almost there. It won't be long before the Ziani will negotiate minor roads independently as well as motorways.'

She refocused back to the car. 'I'm not a good passenger, so my stress levels rise in the car. What about linking a person's stress and comfort indicators to the car? So if someone is nervous, then the car would adjust the speeds, acceleration and braking. With several people in the car, it could produce a compromise.' She studied his face. 'What do you think?'

He beamed and his eyes crinkled at the corners. 'Brilliant! Talk to Dan about the integration but think it through and we'll arrange a quiet time together so you can explain it in more detail.'

'Okay, Aaron.'

Ambiguity again. Was he referring to a meeting in the office just between the two of them, or did he have a different quiet location in mind? Until now, she'd only thought of him as her boss. What about the man? A tricky question which required some serious consideration, but she would press on with the best opportunity she had ever received although the nervous tension it gave her resulted in pounding headaches which only laying the dark, with a joint, could solve.

22

Sadie wearily parked her bicycle in the outhouse of her backyard, as she had come home early after complaining of a headache. Did she have a bug or were the frustrations at work causing her malaise? Everything she wanted to do had been thwarted by Evelyn, whose dismissive and arrogant attitude had worn her down. Her self-esteem was diminishing at a rapid rate.

The excitement of her new idea had crumbled under pressure from Evelyn. She'd had to tell Aaron she hadn't time to develop the details. Previously, she had a close ally in Dan, but she suspected he found her current attitude irritating. Although she tried to stop herself, she constantly moaned.

Within a few minutes, she made herself comfortable on the settee in her small front room. A harrowing headache pounded her forehead and unless she acted, it would intensify. Dark and a joint would help, but that would then become a regular occurrence. She realised the escapism could not be a sustainable future. But what to do?

Evelyn had demanded access to the code so would spot the flaws and the poor documentation. With no love lost between the two of them, Evelyn would speak with Simon and Aaron about her poor standard of work. Then she would be sacked, or would it be better to resign with dignity.

She had adopted a positive approach when taking up her job by being professional and open with people, but she suspected gossiping took place behind her back. Her programme discarded the words and worked on the emotional analysis.

Recording people's speech was wrong and she'd been careful when she had set it up. The words spoken were being streamed to her private cloud. Her software picked up talk on phones and the desktop computers, but most of her interesting readings of emotion came from the microphones in the office.

It had given her some ideas about how to develop her project, as her software would move from the emotional analysis of the individual to investigate relationships. A bubble of excitement welled up, as that would make her work unique. Tapping at the keyboard of her laptop as it rested on her legs, it took only a few clicks to find her private cloud.

Every word spoken over the past week had been recorded and she had not deleted them. The conversations were divided into ten-minute chunks and the files labelled with the names of the people in that conversation. Loading an analysis tool, she pointed it at her private cloud. One remaining task before she could sit back and listen, so she typed in her own name.

The analysis tool would examine the files and pick out several sentences on either side of her name being mentioned. She shouldn't do this and hesitated several times before pressing return, but she was desperate to discover others' opinions of her.

Simon: Is Sadie okay?

Dan: I think so, but she is obsessed by this bloody bracelet.

'Thank you, Dan,' she muttered out loud.

Simon: Yes, I get that feeling.'

Dan: Do you know anything about it?

Simon: About as much as you.

Dan: Do you think Evelyn stole it?

Simon: Why would she?

Dan: Exactly. That's what I keep saying to Sadie.

Sadie frowned at the screen.

Simon: Between you and me. If Sadie doesn't pull herself out of the bad mood and obsession, then I think Aaron will get rid of her.

Sadie drew in a deep breath as she had guessed that outcome, but forced herself to listen.

Dan: Does Aaron think her work is poor?

Simon: No, on the contrary, he thinks it's good, but she is a disruptive influence and it's her fault that the atmosphere in the office is strained.

Dan: 'Do you want me to speak to her, I'd like her to stay.'

'Thank you, Dan.' Tears filled Sadie's eyes as the tension gripped at her temples.

Simon: Yes, that would be helpful.

Simon didn't have enthusiasm in his voice. The file was three days old, but Dan hadn't spoken to her. The situation didn't look good, but at least she understood her position. Should she destroy the voice recordings as they would only depress her even more? She sat staring at the file list for some time. Then one entry caught her attention.

A conversation the previous day between Aaron and Evelyn. She checked the file metadata; it had been recorded from a microphone in Aaron's office. It might be a standard work reference as they were talking about the integration plans or it might be something different? Again, she hesitated before pressing return.

Aaron: 'I want to talk to you about Sadie.'

No reply came from Evelyn.

Aaron: 'How do you get on with her?'

Drawing in a deep breath, Sadie readied herself for the onslaught.

Evelyn: 'That's difficult, Aaron.'

Aaron: 'Come on, Evelyn, I want to know. The atmosphere isn't friendly. Don't you agree.'

Evelyn: 'It's not conducive to good work, I agree.'

A long pause, but she waited patiently.

'I've nothing against Sadie and I like her.'

That came as a surprise.

Aaron: 'What's the problem then?'

Evelyn: 'The bracelet…'

But the strong sound of Aaron's voice cut across Evelyn.

Aaron: 'Did you take the bracelet?'

Evelyn: 'No. By Sadie's own admission, it is cheap. What would I want with it? Do you think I am a kleptomaniac?'

Aaron: 'No, of course not. Now calm down, I've never seen you like this before.'

Evelyn sobbed noisily.

Aaron: 'Here, have a tissue. I'm sorry I didn't mean to upset you. Do I sack Sadie?'

She gulped and waited, holding her breath. This would

be the end for her.

Evelyn: 'No, don't do that. I like her but she's become obsessive about this bracelet. Apart from that, she thinks because I'm the only other female in the office we should be kindred spirits. I'm not like that. I'm sure her idea is to go out together and get drunk. That's not my scene as I don't drink these days. But don't get rid of her.'

The words rattled through her brain and she shook her head in amazement that Evelyn didn't want her to leave. Sadie had the information she needed. Unless she reconsidered, then Aaron would sack her. Dan and Evelyn supported her, even though Dan had been distant recently. Aaron and Simon wanted the mood in the office to return to the former atmosphere of relaxed cooperation. It would be her responsibility to change.

She leaned back and let her mind drift to what she could achieve. There would be hope if she could forget about the bracelet and produce a good standard of work. The others would help her if she struggled. One aspect in the last conversation between Aaron and Evelyn niggled at her, so she replayed it.

As the two voices started, her mind switched to her normal working mode of analysis. It registered! There was something different about the conversation she'd heard. She became excited. This might be the breakthrough she required, so she loaded her emotional analysis software and pointed it at the file.

The analysis graph streamed across her screen. Aaron's voice profile displayed at the top. During the conversation, his speech profile remained close to normal. She picked previous profiles from Aaron. He became irritated, but he remained calm. Most of his annoyance seemed to be directed at Dess. A flicker of mocking amusement crept across her face, as the software that Aaron wanted annoyed him.

Evelyn's profile didn't match her normal mode. She loaded the file before her own name had been mentioned. She didn't speak often in the main office, but when she did, the analysis wavered up and down, a characteristic of nervousness she had discovered in testing on other people.

But when compared to the start of the conversation with Aaron, her profile didn't match. Her voice had lost its nervous edge and remained relaxed, as though she stayed in control when with him. She let the file run through. As soon as Sadie's name had been mentioned, there had been a blip on the analysis profile but not a significant one. Evelyn had been content to talk about Sadie. The mention of the bracelet triggered tension in her voice and it shot off the scale when she mentioned kleptomaniac.

Many emotions skewed the profiles. The most common reason would be lying. In her work she had researched lie detectors and the changing effect on the emotion of the voice. She needed to think differently about Evelyn. Had she been lying when she denied being a thief. Could she find out?

She typed Evelyn's name into Google. It brought up the usual Linkedin business reference. The other day, Dan had made a sarcastic comment about her name. When Evelyn had been first appointed, Simon had introduced her with a double-barrelled name. Evelyn had told them she only used Chumley.

There was a different spelling of Chumley. She typed in Cholmondeley and Evelyn. Still no return. What about the EU regulation which meant names could be removed from searches? She would give it one last go. She picked a search engine from her student days that had often been used for the darker side of the internet.

The name appeared on the screen, Evelyn Cholmondeley-Smythe, in a newspaper article about a high-flying computer student who had been arrested for shoplifting while drunk. She guessed the article referred to Evelyn.

Sadie sat back and sighed. Evelyn had a problem. She had taken the bracelet and must have a difficult past life trying to cope. She couldn't imagine living with that type of mental health problem. The discovery changed her outlook. She would not snipe at Evelyn. Her behaviour had been explained.

She never touched alcohol and avoided friendship because of her compulsion to steal.

23

Aaron settled in his chair. Ahmed closed the door as he entered. This would not be a good meeting. His friend gave him a perfunctory handshake, but the frown never lifted.

'Face reality, Aaron, you took on the best, but the team is weak.' Ahmed slapped the flat of his hand on the table for emphasis. 'The ideas are interesting, but the development has been poor. It's four weeks since you and Dan met Emmanuel. The progress report you sent him shows little that's new. Although impressive at first, there are no positive follow-ups.'

'I know!' Aaron rubbed a hand over his aching head and stared at the composed figure of Ahmed sitting across from him. A tinge of envy touched him. Ahmed was rich and successful. He suspected people thought the same about him, but it wasn't true. The business needed to succeed so he could continue with his luxury lifestyle.

Ahmed's voice broke into his thoughts. 'Promoting your cause has been a misjudgement on my behalf. If we are to progress, the team needs to be enlarged with a greater range of skills, which would contribute more experience.'

'That won't work. The existing ones will walk out and then we'll be back to square one.'

Ahmed tapped a finger in a staccato rhythm on the table. 'Also, I haven't forgotten about that email problem six weeks ago. Since then, I've been nervous about writing emails.'

A puzzled expression furrowed Aaron's brow. Ahmed had mentioned the email problem at every meeting. Why was he so paranoid about it? What did he have to hide? Ahmed placed his hand on the papers in front of him. 'Are you sure you can deliver the final product with the correct security and integrity?'

'You can rest your mind, Ahmed, the whole issue of access to the systems is much tighter.'

'The reason for coming to see you today is to decide the best way forward and my inclination is to curtail the funding.' The words cut through Aaron like a knife. Ahmed's expression became unyielding. 'I fear I'm throwing good money after bad and there will never be a return. Basically, if you ever want my help again in funding, then you need to get me out of this mess.'

'That's harsh, I've my money invested as well.'

'That's not my concern. You've picked the wrong staff to deliver the ideas. It would have been better to have one ideas person and more skills at implementing.'

Aaron straightened his back. 'I thought we were in this together but you're implying that I tried to con you.'

Ahmed spoke through gritted teeth, 'Let's face it, it's a mess. Whatever way we look at it, the venture will lose money. How can we minimalise our losses, unless you are convinced you can market the triangle of projects and make a success of them?'

Aaron stood and paced his office. He stared at the parked cars. Losing his money was not an option for him. He had to keep Ahmed and his investment on board. Attempting to ease his tension, he rolled his shoulders as his mind raced through a range of possibilities. 'What about a return in a restricted way?'

'I don't understand?'

'We focus the triangle of products on the Ziani and bring in other home and environment factors later.'

'But do the team know enough about the car?'

'No, but we could let them drive our cars. All four are fascinated with the Ziani, but they can't afford one themselves. As they are technical people, they want to understand.'

'Could we trust them to drive?'

'We can monitor them anytime with the existing apps.'

Ahmed shook his head.

'You came here today wanting a way forward. A restricted project could be delivered quickly. You need to arrange the insurance on your car.'

Ahmed looked unhappy, but he nodded.

'I'll use Evelyn as our guinea pig, as she's already asked if she can have a drive.' Ahmed packed up his computer, put on his coat and reached the door. 'It's not a brilliant idea but I'm willing to go with it. Just remember there's no more money.'

24

Sadie drew in a deep breath as she sat next to Evelyn who typed away. The afternoon had been an intense exchange as many changes were required. With a struggle to maintain her positive approach to Evelyn, she inwardly sighed as the woman had problems. She must be a complex character if she can cope with her inner devils of the compulsions to steal and maintain the outer appearances of amazing technological understanding.

'This is the code.' Evelyn swept the cursor across a large expanse of the program. 'Can you update it? The emotional categories need revision.'

Fidgeting in her chair with a tight expression she'd tried several times to change Evelyn's approach to her work. Her mind raced through more possible arguments. Why wouldn't she understand her point of view?

'With these changes, Evelyn, it's difficult to progress the attributes I wish to implement.'

'We are struggled against deadlines, we need the changes to make progress, otherwise Ahmed will cut off the supply of money.'

Rubbing the back of her neck, Sadie attempted to relieve the tension and to suppress her rising hysteria. She opened her mouth to argue her point but closed it again, the words remaining unspoken. 'It's late and I need time to consider your suggestions, but I can't cope with any more today so I'm going home.'

Evelyn snorted with disgust. 'If you must.'

Sadie collected her papers, picked up her notebook and jammed them into her bag while Evelyn glared at her through narrowed eyes. 'Before you go.'

She shoved back her chair in readiness to leave. 'What is it?'

'The three apps are live again. Dess is working and I'll contact the others by email. We can start monitoring the feedback again.' Evelyn's arrogant voice cut through Sadie, whose shoulders drooped as she looked at the floor. 'I've made a start on the integration on the new Dess.'

Sadie would not prolong the conversation. She picked up her rucksack and put it on over the top of her fluorescent jacket. She didn't delay because Evelyn could ask for another piece of urgent work. Exhausted and frustrated, she would leave before receiving any further requests. The sympathy for Evelyn had worn thin, but Sadie's job with TechMatt hinged on her attitude, not her technical brilliance.

The cycle ride home in the rain had been slow with her mind awash with negative thoughts about Evelyn. She lurched into her flat, dripping wet, tired and tense. A peaceful evening beckoned.

'Hi, Sadie.' The tinny voice echoed in the kitchen. 'Did you have a good day?'

She blew out her cheeks. 'No, Dess, I didn't. Evelyn is too demanding, she's a thorough slave driver. Also, she never smiles.' Reaching her arms above her head, she stretched to relieve her stiffness. Wallowing in the movement's luxuriousness, she regretted her outburst as Evelyn could monitor Dess's recordings. 'Your voice is stressful, which shouldn't be the case.'

Sadie stopped, and with wide eyes, stared at the speaker. 'That's not a normal reply. Why shouldn't I sound stressed after my day which has been long and hard?'

'A few days ago, you stated you had grown to respect Evelyn.'

'Hang on, Dess.'

'What is it?'

'Evelyn turned off the system.'

'Only for responses, I still recorded.'

She froze as anger coursed through her. Why had Evelyn been so devious? What had she hoped to achieve by eavesdropping on their conversations?

'We should have been told. Send Evelyn a message and ask her why she continued with recording.'

'There is annoyance in your voice. Before I send the message, I will let you reconsider. Such messages sent in haste can be regretted later.'

'Don't argue with me. Send the bloody message!'

'I'll review the matter with you when you have relaxed. Please calm down, your physiological readings are outside of your target range.'

'This is too much!' She shook her fist at the speaker as her cheeks flared with heat. 'I will not be ordered around by a damned machine.' Slumping into the chair with an exasperated breath, irritation rifled through her body. The only person who could help her through the next few weeks would be Dan.

25

Dan packed away his work earlier than normal. He needed a few beers to relax. The office atmosphere had intensified as Evelyn ruled the decision making as though she was the boss. He had coped and had received a smile from her. But his stress was rising. The job was a big opportunity. Being part of a small team delivering a leading project would ensure money in the future. He would persevere.

'Dan, can I have a word before you leave.' Aaron emerged from his office as Dan switched off his computer. With concern at the cool tone of Aaron's voice, he gave a shiver. He had also been working late many evenings. Unusually, Aaron hadn't slumped on a chair for a general chat.

Nodding, he followed Aaron to his office. A flood of anxiety swept through him. Why did he want to speak? Had Evelyn been moaning about his poor computing skills?

He dropped himself onto the seat near Aaron's desk.

'How's progress?'

'Not bad.' He attempted to choose his words with care. 'Evelyn is demanding about the changes.'

'Do her requests make sense?'

'Yes, but it's hard to satisfy her and to keep developing my app.'

Aaron's narrowed eyes searched his face. 'She's talented.

Behind that unsmiling and solemn exterior lurks an intelligent woman.'

Dan ran a hand through his tangled hair and a stab of uneasiness swarmed through him. This conversation was taking the form of an interrogation. It was common knowledge that Aaron was having an affair with her, so he was bound to side with her in any disagreement.

'I don't doubt her ability.'

Aaron rested his elbows on the table and steepled his fingers. A smile flickered. 'Evelyn told me of good progress with the integration which will lead to an impressive product.' He leaned back in his chair and his eyes flashed with excitement.

Criticising Evelyn was a dangerous course to take, but he needed to voice his worries. He couldn't pretend that everything was great. Telling the truth was the best way forward. With a deep breath, he would voice his opinion. 'It's developing but I have concerns.'

An uneasy silence greeted his remark. Outside a motorbike engine roared. Dan swallowed dryly, unable to wet his parched throat. A sudden frown of suspicion coupled with irritation crossed Aaron's forehead. 'Why? Is it flaky?'

'No, the code is robust.' Dan fidgeted as his forehead beaded with sweat. 'It's the direction the integration is taking.'

'Explain!'

The slightest problem made Aaron lose his cool. With a silent groan, Dan forced himself to concentrate, hoping that he would not vent his anger.

Aaron's hard stare bored into him. With trepidation, he wanted to choose the right words. 'Sadie rang me earlier to say that Dess is answering back.'

Aaron laughed and the tension on his face evaporated as his eyes twinkled with amusement.

'It annoyed Sadie, as she hadn't programmed it that way. In her mind, Dess is supposed to be supportive and helpful.' He fixed Aaron, 'Have you found any problems with Dess?'

Aaron shook his head. 'I didn't know that it was live again.'

'Hello, Aaron. I'm live again. The electronic voice echoed around the room. I intended to let you know on your way home.' Aaron stared at his computer speaker and rubbed his chin.

'Dess, you normally only come to life when you are called or have a reminder set.'

'That's right, Aaron, but Evelyn has made me more pro-active, so I can monitor what goes on. Then I can volunteer to help if it's within my capabilities.'

'Interesting development; I suppose it takes a step away from other systems that wait to be called.'

'Listen to this, Aaron. Dess.'

'Yes, Dan. What can I do for you?'

'What's on my shopping list?'

'We discussed that recently.'

Aaron gave the speaker a concentrated stare.

'I know, remind me.'

'Pasta, baking potatoes, lettuce, tomatoes and cucumber. Do you want the exact amounts?'

'No. What happened to the bacon and oven chips I asked you to put on the list.'

'Your lifestyle measurements are not compatible with bacon and chips.' The tinny voice echoed around the room.

'Why have you added salad ingredients? I didn't ask for them.'

'You've had them before so you must like them.' He grinned at Aaron.

'You seemed dissatisfied with my advice, Dan.'

'How do you know? Explain the technical details, Dess.'

'I recognise the facial expression from camera three in Aaron's office. I can tell from the slight rise in decibels in your voice and the slight lengthening of words.'

Aaron snapped, 'Turn yourself off, Dess. Go back to the state where you only listen for your name. Do not record.'

'Yes, Aaron.'

'There's something else. Dess, before you obey Aaron, tell me about the new playlist you created for me.'

'Do you want me to explain again?'

'Yes.'

'Music is one of your favourite activities, so I wanted to be helpful. I interrogated your Amazon Echo at home and your phone playlist and your car playlist. The systems supplied me with the frequencies of plays. From that, I mixed a playlist from your favourites and music with similar criteria from Spotify. I didn't ask you before, but I see you examined the list. Did I make a good choice?'

'Yes, Dess. A quite exceptional one. Follow Aaron's instructions and turn yourself off.'

They fell into silence and stared at each other.

Finally, Aaron rubbed his face, 'It's a surprise Dess has become proactive.'

Dan gave a wry smile. 'Proactive I could cope with but it's trying to take me over.'

Aaron stared with worried eyes and chewed at his bottom lip. 'Do you think it's a one-off?'

He shook his head. 'No, Sadie told me Dess answered her back and wouldn't send a message of complaint to Evelyn.'

Aaron groaned, 'I don't see how we could launch this.'

'We've connected it up to everything as part of the plan.'

Aaron fidgeted in his chair. 'I understand that, but the system wants to burrow into every corner and might well be able to find links. It could become out of control.'

'I agree. We're building a white elephant that no one is going to want.' He studied his boss. Could he extricate himself from the mess of giving Evelyn total control? Probably not, but at least he would get a good reference for his next job.

26

Aaron offered the car to those in the office to help on the restricted project. Dan and Sadie had been for an evening drive. Evelyn had requested a weekend to visit her parents, so he settled in the passenger seat of the Ziani next to Evelyn, who would drive him home. A mixture of irritation and disappointment coursed through him as Evelyn made herself comfortable and fastened her seatbelt.

Throughout the recent staff meetings, she had refused to acknowledge the crisis which her integration program had caused. Infatuation with her had played a part because he had taken her side in the discussions about the project. In retrospect, he should have considered all options and maintained a balanced view. He hadn't suggested another liaison out of work as he concentrated on salvaging the business. It would be time for fun and leisure when the crisis had been resolved.

'Thanks for letting me have it for the weekend.' Evelyn's eyes flashed and a small smile crossed her face.

Tightening his jaw, he lowered his head and avoided eye contact. 'I've work to complete, but I've no reason to visit the office. Candice is away for a long weekend's hen party, so I will have peace at home. I don't need a car but if I do, I can use Candice's.'

A broad smile crossed her face. 'I'm visiting my parents on the coast. My dad will love the car.'

Aaron wanted to avoid talking about the project, as this was not a good opportunity. His mind swirled with his business problems. He had an idea about re-funding if Ahmed withdrew. The quiet weekend would allow him to work through the idea before talking to anyone else.

As the car pulled on to the drive outside of Aaron's house, he gave a small silent sigh. 'I'll give you my notes about the user interface for the app.'

'Okay.' Evelyn slid from the car and followed Aaron towards the house. He switched on the hall light.

'It's quiet. Has Candice left?'

Taking his time to reply, he hoped his face did not show the lie. 'No, the hen party is flying out later.' Preferring not to be alone with her as after the weekend he might sack her, he would spend Saturday examining her work, then decide.

Aaron picked up a folder from the table in the hall and handed it to her. 'You'll need to read my notes.'

Nodding, she stared up at him with an expectant look on her face. 'My parents aren't expecting me until late this evening, it's only a couple of hours so I don't have to rush.'

Flicking his eyes over Evelyn, he forced a smile. 'I'd love you to stay, but Candice might return.' Leaning forward, he kissed her on the cheek. Making no comment, she tilted her head to one side studying his expression.

He watched her depart as the drive gates opened automatically. He hoped his ploy had worked, as Candice had flown out this morning and would be preparing for a binge in Prague.

27

Candice leaned back in the comfortable armchair and closed her eyes. The luxurious hotel room had been decorated in shades of cream with a huge king bed as the central feature.

The weekend in Prague might be the last of her luxuries, unless she could help Aaron out of the mess he had created. The monetary situation would be dire if the financial plug was pulled next week. The hen weekend wasn't a sensible idea as she needed to concentrate on keeping her life on an even keel with plenty of money as she had no intention of returning to a working day.

A shiver of apprehension pulsed through her at the thought of working from nine to five. She had an incentive and pressed the button on her phone.

She gave a nervous smile, 'Hello, Candice.'

'Ahmed, we need to talk.'

'I'd prefer more than talk.'

Rolling her shoulders, she pressed her lips together in determination. 'Possibly, but I need answers.'

'Such as?'

'Will you cancel the finance for the project?'

A derisive laugh echoed down the phone, 'Of course.'

'Does Aaron have any chance at next week's meeting?'

'Negligible. He needs to show substantial progress, so my fellow investors have confidence. It need not be finished but there should be a clear demonstration of the project's substance, but it's all pie-in-the-sky ideas.' A note of contempt had crept into his voice.

Gripping the phone, her mind raced, searching for answers. No obvious solution presented itself.

'When we first heard Dess, we were impressed. Time has moved on. I want to be equally astounded next week and if that happens, then the money could continue. But it won't...'

He stopped talking. The silence lengthened. 'Are you still there, Ahmed?'

'Yes, I'm thinking about why you have rung me.'

'Only for a chat.'

'No. I understand the reason for the call. Aaron's finances must be in a bad way and I guess that even your house is mortgaged up to the hilt. If the project goes pear-shaped you can say hello to a small semi-detached.' His voice was dispassionate. 'You never ring me, so you want to get back into my good books again so you can abandon the sinking ship. Isn't that right?'

Once again, the silence lengthened. She needed to keep him talking, as he'd already confessed to being infatuated with her. 'Do you think that I'm that fickle, Ahmed?'

'I know you too well, Candice, a relationship would be on my terms as you've told me you prefer Aaron, so I'd be second best.'

An idea spun into her mind. 'Have you deliberately encouraged Aaron to go beyond his capabilities, so that you can get at me.'

'You are not as daft as you appear.' The line went dead.

Her call hadn't worked, as she'd expected that Ahmed would be easy to manipulate.

Jumping as the phone rang, she didn't recognise the number but pressed the answer button. 'Hello.'

'Hello, Candice. This is Evelyn.'

'Hi.' She didn't wish to speak to her, but it could be important, as she'd never rung before.

'Aaron has let me have the Ziani for the weekend.'

'I know.'

'I dropped him at your house about twenty minutes ago. I've tried to ring but can't reach him. He commented that you would be home soon. I'd forgot to tell him I will return the car on Sunday afternoon.'

'I'm in a hotel in Prague. I flew out this morning so I can't pass on your message personally.'

'Okay. Sorry to trouble you, bye.'

What a strange phone call, but she dismissed it as she left her bedroom to join her friends. It would be a long drunken weekend, but she would sober up next week and deal with

Aaron and the others at TechMatt. No one would take away her lifestyle and income.

28

Candice's weekend in Prague had been nonstop partying, which had pushed her financial problems to the back of her mind. But in the few moments of clarity, she vowed she would take control of Aaron and TechMatt. The taxi pulled into the drive outside of her home. The security lights illuminated the large, detached house. Rubbing her hand across her pounding forehead, she plodded across the gravel towards the front door. The drinking sessions had been heavy.

A good night's sleep and she'd be fine. The thought of curling up under a cosy duvet and closing her eyes appealed to her tired body. She would need an alert mind to deal with the problems that faced her. Ahmed's devious behaviour had shocked her. She found it hard to forgive him for undermining Aaron, his best friend. Whether she could turn the project around on her own would be doubtful, so she would need help. Who from TechMatt would be prepared to help?

Fumbling in her bag for the key, her mind ploughed through the issues. Ahmed had self-interest in his mind, so she couldn't trust him. Aaron wouldn't listen to her, so she needed someone else. Someone to lean on who she could trust.

The mini-Cooper wasn't parked in its usual spot on the drive, so she guessed Aaron had taken it as Evelyn had borrowed the Ziani for the weekend. The strange phone call from her flashed back into her mind. Her message had been that she was returning the Ziani this afternoon. She flicked on the lights in the darkened house.

Too much alcohol over the weekend had left her lethargic. The alcohol during the flight had given her the boost needed to deal with the short meeting she'd arranged on the way home. Although informative, it didn't present the complete answer.

She wandered through to the kitchen and poured herself a glass of chilled water from the dispenser in the large American fridge. Perching at the island breakfast bar, she sipped the water and enjoyed the sensation of the cool liquid gliding down her throat. She pursed her lips and dispelled the negative thoughts from her mind. Having devised a plan in the quiet moments over the weekend, she was ready for implementation

Picking up her phone, she found the number and pressed the call button. 'Simon, this is Candice, we need to talk.' Her hand clenched the phone in a vice-like grip. 'The situation is desperate.'

'Yes, I know. It's Aaron's fault.' The tension in his voice was unmistakable. 'He supported Evelyn, and she's taken the project in the wrong direction.'

'I agree!' She flapped her hand in the air in irritation 'But apportioning blame will not resolve the problem. We will be in a mess if the business fails.'

'Why will you be? I don't understand.'

'Aaron has invested too much of his own money and he's revealed that our house is at risk.'

'I thought Ahmed would lose out as he's the money man.'

Her eyes narrowed, and she tapped her painted nails in an irritated rhythm on the breakfast bar. 'For reasons I won't go into, Ahmed has encouraged Aaron to spend too much money. The amount that Ahmed has invested is small compared to his fortune. He can lose it without even noticing. Aaron can't.'

A lengthy pause followed her revelation. Candice waited; her plan must succeed. 'I didn't realise how serious the situation had become. Dan is expecting the worst and so am I.'

'That's why I want to talk with you as I've a plan, but it needs your help.'

Simon's reply was immediate, 'If it's likely to work, then I'll try it. What are you thinking?'

'Can we meet?'

'Yes, but tell me more.'

'We need to persuade Aaron to kick Evelyn out of the door at the earliest opportunity.'

'Why will that help?'

'You could take over the integration with Dan and Sadie. Would you be able to make the integration appealing to the moneymen?'

'It's not as simple as that.'

'Why not?'

'Evelyn has set up a complex system which only she understands.'

'That's my point, Simon, it's too complicated to amend.'

'I don't understand.'

'We take the three original parts of the triangle before Evelyn became involved. You must have separate copies of them.'

'Yes, we have.'

'Then the three of you build a simple integration.'

'Timescales are short.'

'Can you think of a better solution?' She pressed the phone closer to her ear as the tension in her body increased.

'No. I don't have a better idea, although it probably won't work, but I'm sure that Dan and Sadie will support me if I try.'

'That's good, so you're on board.' An exhausted sigh escaped from her lips. Perhaps her plan might work.

'Yes, providing you can get rid of Evelyn, but Aaron won't agree.'

'Leave him to me.' Her jaw clenched. Aaron would do what she instructed. A few home truths about his behaviour would be needed. She refocused on the conversation. 'I want a clear idea of a way forward. It's important that I understand.'

'Why?'

'Never mind.' She sucked in her breath as she tried to keep her voice level. 'Can we meet tonight and go through the possibilities?'

'What about Aaron?'

'He's not here. He must have taken my car, as it's not on the drive. I've been away with friends so I can use them as an excuse. I'll explain I've been with them this evening as we extended the celebrations.'

'Okay, where shall we meet?'

'At the gym. That will appear normal. Several of my friends work there. Evelyn intended leaving the Ziani here this afternoon. It will have parked itself in the garage. It's crucial we meet.'

'I'll go there now. Come when you can.'

Closing the call, she became fired up with her plan so would go immediately. Simon would need prompting for a viable solution. Impatience gripped her. She put on her coat, picked up her bag, and opened the front door.

29

Flicking at her phone, she opened the app to summon the Ziani from the garage. The muffled whirr from the garage door opening carried across the evening air. The security lights failed to illuminate the area as she strode to the garage, keeping to one side to allow the car to manoeuvre. She tutted in annoyance. The bulb must have blown.

The warmth from the garage spread over her from the opened door. The gun metal grey glistened from the street-lights as the Ziani emerged from the dark garage. She didn't turn on the garage light and waited for the car to fully emerge.

Her eyes widened and her hand flew to her mouth. She wanted to scream, but no sound emerged from her gaping jaw. Rooted to the spot, she closed her eyes, telling herself that her mind was playing tricks. A ghastly trick of the light, but her vivid imagination had created a nightmare image.

Taking a deep breath to calm the pounding of her heart, her whole body trembled as she stepped into the garage and, with a shaking hand, groped the wall for the light switch. The fluorescent tube flicked into life. In the distance, a siren wailed. Then quietness fell. The Ziani had stopped moving. Uneasiness crept over her. An inside rational voice kept repeating, there's nothing wrong. You're overreacting. With a trembling finger, she located the Ziani app on her mobile and flicked on the car lights.

From semi-darkness, the headlights and interior lights of the car illuminated the area. With trepidation, she forced herself to approach the driver's door. A nightmare scene.

Her head swirled and she leaned against the car to stop herself from falling. 'Oh, my God! What's happened!' Blood. The bright lights reflected a congealed red mass. Blood everywhere. Dark crimson patterns streaked the white leather seats. Nausea welled up inside her.

With desperation, she forced herself to look again. Evelyn, in the driver's seat but half slumped across the passenger side with her limp white hand resting through the steering wheel.

Evelyn's bloodied pale face rested on the passenger's seat, so she had no doubt about the identity.

'Evelyn!' she whispered. Her legs gave way as dizziness gripped her. She swayed. Leaning against the car, she pulled open the driver's door. Was Evelyn breathing, or was she dead? She needed to find out. As she leant in, her legs buckled and she crumpled to the ground. She lay on the hard gravel, her mind swirling and her breathing shallow. Fighting the faintness, the cold November breeze cooled her sweating forehead.

Fright filled her body. She wanted to run away, to scream, to distance herself from the nightmare, but her body wouldn't respond. Sobbing, she stared wildly around. Her chest grew tight and bile rose in her throat. Her bag had fallen. On hands and knees, she grappled towards it. Sitting on the ground, she propped her back against the car and, with trembling fingers, pressed 999.

30

Aaron swung the car onto the road where he lived. Blue flashing lights illuminating the night sky drenched his headlights. After a garbled message from Candice about an accident, he'd raced the Mini Cooper across Sheffield in a panic. A policeman stood in the gateway and raised his hand to stop him. He wound down the window. 'I'm Aaron Matthews. I live here. What's happening? Where's my wife? Is she okay?'

He glanced across at his Ziani, illuminated by floodlights on the gravel driveway. 'What's happened to Evelyn? Why is the car covered in blood?' The questions tumbled out. Clutching the steering wheel as though his life depended on it, fear twisted in the pit of his stomach and his heart raced. Sweat drenched his body.

With every second that passed, the terror increased. He must reach Candice.

No sense of urgency emanated from the policeman, who blocked his way. He didn't answer any of the questions but stared at Aaron with a grave expression. The policeman spoke into his radio, waited for a reply and then pointed to a parking space along the road. With an overwhelming sense of dread, Aaron had no option but to follow the instructions, as he was desperate to enter the house and be with Candice.

He roared down the road and flung the car into the space. As he jumped out of the car, a policewoman waited, 'Come this way, sir, I will escort you through the scene.' In a daze, he stumbled up the road towards his house.

Three police cars filled his drive. The Ziani was parked in front of the open garage. Several people in white coveralls swarmed the area. Uniformed police with crackling radios stood guard. He ran with stumbling strides to the front door, though his legs didn't want to cooperate.

The officer led him into his own lounge. Candice huddled on the sofa next to a policewoman. Her pale face and haunted eyes clocked his arrival. 'Candice!' he choked.

'I can't stand up. I'll faint again.' Aaron rushed to her.

The police officer moved to another chair, allowing him to sit next to her. He threw his arms around her shoulders and drew her towards him. Rocking her gently backwards and forwards, her whole body shook.

'Terrible!' Wracking sobs consumed her. He kissed the top of her head. Worry coursed through him as he had never seen Candice in such a hysterical state. She must have had a terrible fright. Although a million questions circled around his mind, they would wait until she had calmed enough to talk. For now, he continued to rock her gently, hoping the motion would help.

The words, 'In there,' caught his attention.

Two people entered the room. 'I'm Detective Sergeant Jane Mulgrave from Sheffield police. She showed her warrant card. This is Doctor Henderson, who has come to see your wife.' Aaron nodded and released his grip of Candice but kept one comforting arm around her shoulder. Candice lifted her tear-stained face and dabbed at her eyes with a soggy tissue. A shuddering groan escaped her lips.

'Perhaps Mr Matthews you would come with me to give me background information while the doctor assists your wife.'

Candice grabbed at his arm, 'Don't go.'

Aaron squeezed his wife's shoulder and eased himself from the sofa.

'We will be in the kitchen, so your husband will be nearby when you need him.'

Candice drew in a stuttered gasp, 'Don't you want to talk to me?'

'All in good time. Let the doctor help you first.' The doctor had already positioned himself next to Candice and held her wrist.

Aaron rubbed his forehead as he glanced anxiously at his wife's tear-stained face. With reluctance, he twisted away and headed towards the kitchen with the Sergeant following.

'I'll tell you what I can, Sergeant, but I've only just arrived home.'

'I'm aware of that. At this stage, it is mainly background information.'

Slumping onto a breakfast bar stool, he stared down at his hands and absentmindedly twisted his wedding ring. His chest rose and fell with rapid breaths. 'Are you okay, sir?'

He lifted his head and rubbed a hand over his forehead. 'It's a shock to come home and find my wife in such a condition and to learn that Evelyn has had an accident. Did she crash the car? Candice didn't give details but informed me there was a lot of blood.'

The Sergeant didn't smile. 'Shall I make you a cup of tea while we talk, you look like you need one.' She glanced around, located the kettle and with her back towards Aaron, filled it with water.

He fidgeted on the bar stool. 'As Candice mentioned a lot of blood, I assume Evelyn is badly injured.' The Sergeant took her time and busied herself locating mugs, tea and milk while the kettle boiled. He watched her every move. Lines of stress formed on his forehead and his fingers tapped a rhythm on the work surface.

The Sergeant placed a mug of tea on the breakfast bar. She settled herself onto a bar stool on the opposite side and removed a notebook and pen from her pocket, placing these onto the work surface with irritating precision. Annoyance at the delays made his stomach contract into a tight ball.

'When the ambulance arrived, the paramedics found her alive so took her to hospital. She has a serious head injury and they were not optimistic she would survive. The chances improve if she reaches hospital.'

'Yes, I understand about her injuries, but what happened? Did she crash the car?' His voice shook with frustration.

The Sergeant ignored his questions and with a sombre expression, 'I believe you employed Evelyn.'

Aaron sipped his tea as he mulled over her statement. His head spun. How had she come to that conclusion? Her mouth twisted into a knowing smile. 'Your wife managed to tell the first officer on the scene that she worked for your company.'

'Yes, she has been with me for several months. I own a new IT start-up business.'

'Can you tell me her full name?'

'Evelyn Cholmondeley-Smythe but she normally used the name Evelyn Chumley.'

'Any reason?'

'Only convenience.'

'Do you own the Ziani?'

'Yes, she had borrowed it for the weekend.'

'Do your staff normally use such a prestigious car?'

He shook his head. 'We intend developing an application for the car. I only have four employees, so I have offered them the chance to drive it for a short period. I've been busy this weekend so as Evelyn had planned a trip to see her parents, I agreed she could take the car.'

'When had she planned to return it?'

'During Sunday, no specific time.'

The Sergeant wrote a few words in her notebook. 'Can you tell me your movements over the weekend please?'

'I've been here throughout the weekend.'

'Except for the past few hours?'

'I went out about five hours ago.'

'May I ask why?'

His stomach tightened and he shifted his position on the bar stool. 'I'd been working over the weekend and needed to talk to a member of staff.'

'On a Sunday evening? Is that normal?'

'Yes, Sergeant, we are a small company with a dedicated staff and are near to the launch of a product, so we work long hours. One of my staff suggested a new idea and I wanted to understand more about it. We often work over the weekend.'

'Did that include Evelyn?'

'Yes, all five of us.'

'Who did you visit this evening?'

'I met Sadie Joiner.'

The Sergeant didn't hesitate. 'Do you know where your wife intended going tonight?'

He shook his head. 'She'd been away for the weekend. I didn't know she'd arrived home as I didn't expect her back until tomorrow.'

A discreet cough came from the doorway. The Sergeant glanced in that direction. 'Yes, doctor?'

'May I have a word?'

As the Sergeant clicked the door shut, Aaron closed his eyes and summoned a deep breath. The questions had come thick and fast. Turning his head a fraction, he strained to listen to the muffled conversation.

Within minutes, the Sergeant returned and settled on the bar stool. Without any preamble, 'The doctor has identified alcohol on your wife's breath. Would you normally expect her to have been drinking at this time?'

'I can understand the reason for the question. Normally no, although we might have a drink later in the evening with a meal, but she'd been away on a hen weekend. I assume she has carried on drinking on the plane home.'

'Which raises the next point. If Mrs Matthews had been drinking, why would she decide to go out again so soon after arriving home.'

'I do not know. Why not ask her?'

'The doctor has administered a sedative and she has fallen asleep.'

'Unless you have other requirements of me, I shall sit with my wife.'

'We will wish to speak with you tomorrow. Do you have any plans?'

He shook his head, 'I shall be either at home or in the office.'

'We will find you.'

31

Simon shivered with worry; he hadn't slept. Candice had never arrived at the gym. The strange phone call from her had unnerved him. From appearing to have a nominal role in the business, she implied she would become the central figure.

Last night on the phone her husky tones had disappeared. The sharp voice showed business acumen. After waiting at the gym for over an hour, he had sent several texts, but had received no reply.

Consumed with a mixture of concern and curiosity, he drove past her house. As he had approached, the police had waved him on. Her house was illuminated by blue flashing lights. He hadn't stopped to ask what had happened. Had Candice met with an accident? His mind had swirled with speculation throughout the long, restless night.

Sitting alone in Aaron's office, he had been summoned to a meeting. The text read, Meeting 0900. Urgent. Serious.

Candice? What had happened to her? The previous anticipation of being in bed with her clouded his thoughts. Violent nightmare scenarios that had invaded his mind overnight swam back into his thoughts. He fidgeted with a chill shiver.

The outside door of the office opened and footsteps approached. He glanced at his wrist, eight fifty-five. His Fitbit buzzed. His readings were too high. Tension, clandestine meetings and lack of sleep agitated him.

Deep, calming breaths didn't reduce the readings.

Sadie bustled into the office and dropped her fluorescent coat and helmet in the corner. 'What's the reason for the meeting?'

'I don't know.' He wouldn't speculate. Distancing himself from yesterday evening would be his best ploy.

Sadie settled at the meeting table. 'I rang Dan, and he had the same message, but he didn't know either.'

Simon refrained from mentioning the blue lights at Aaron's house. The reason for being in the area would be difficult to explain. The local radio news this morning had cited a police incident in that part of town. They expected to make a statement during the morning but had issued no further details.

The outside door slammed; footsteps thudded across the hard floor. Dan hurried into the office and plonked himself next to Sadie. He scanned their faces. 'Any news?' They shook their heads. He scowled, leaned back, his bushy eyebrows forming a dark bar across his face. 'We will be searching for a new job in a few minutes.'

Neither replied.

They sat in silence. Simon's hands shook so he hid them in his lap.

The outside door closed. A shiver ran through him. Aaron would have news, but did he want to hear it? Sweat ran down his back. The glance at the unkempt and unshaved Aaron as he entered the office increased his shaking. Only a devastating incident affecting Candice would cause the transformation to Aaron.

Aaron joined the three at the table. He took a deep breath and his haunted eyes scanned the room, 'I have bad news.' His bleak voice echoed in the still office, 'Evelyn is critically ill in hospital, she's in a coma, her chances of survival are slim.'

'My God! Poor Evelyn.' Sadie's hand flew to her mouth.

Simon forced his features to show outward composure. Relief flooded him that it wasn't Candice. Evelyn, Aaron's mistress, had been involved in a terrible accident. Ensuring his voice remained steady, 'What happened?' He attempted to link Evelyn's condition to the blue flashing police lights at Aaron's house.

Aaron rubbed his face with both hands. His eyes were wide and troubled. 'Candice found her with serious head injuries.' Silence followed the revelation as they stared at him with confusion across their faces.

Dan stroked his beard. 'Candice?' The single word split through the silence as though asking a multitude of questions. Simon exhaled with relief as Dan had asked about her.

Aaron's pale face leeched of any remaining colour. 'Candice found Evelyn in the Ziani at our house slumped in the driver's seat covered in blood.' He looked away and pinched the bridge of his nose as he closed his eyes. They waited in silence for him to continue. 'We didn't know she had arrived back with the car as it had been parked in the garage. Candice wanted to use the car and made the discovery.'

Without hesitation, Sadie blurted, 'What happened? Why was she covered in blood?'

A wince of discomfort flickered across Aaron's face. 'The police have given no details, but they have updated me this morning on her condition. Candice is upset, but I wanted to tell you in person. The police asked me to say that they will wish to speak to you, so can you make yourselves available? Especially you, Sadie.'

Sadie gulped and a rosy glow spread across her cheeks from the sudden mention of her name, then the colour drained rapidly from her face. Simon and Dan stared at her with wide eyed fascination. Why would the police want to speak to Sadie?

Had Candice told the police she was on her way to meet him. What would he say to them? The wrong answer and they would arrest him. What a mess! Why did he have to become involved with Candice?

Aaron's voice brought his attention back to the meeting. 'I rang Sadie to talk about her project and agreed to meet her in Meadowhall last night.' Aaron's flat and weary voice was edged with anxiety. 'After I had left home, Candice arrived and made the discovery.'

Simon wanted to deflect any focus away from him. 'I'm sorry to hear about Evelyn. What do we do now?'

Aaron flicked his head as if coming back to reality. 'I'm not sure if the meeting with Ahmed will take place later in the week. It will be problematic, but we need to carry on with the project as normal.'

'Concentration will be difficult.' Sadie shuffled in her chair.

'I understand, but we will have to do our best.'

Sadie nodded, 'I'll tidy my code for Dess.'

Silence pervaded the office; they were reluctant to move. Simon attempted to gather his thoughts and pull himself together. After all, he was the team leader. He hoped Candice would contact him today. Dan and Sadie would need his support and encouragement to focus on their work. Despite his problems, it would be time to step up to his team leader role. About to push back his chair, the computer in Aaron's office booted to come out of standby. He hesitated as the disc hummed into life. Four pairs of eyes focused on the computer; lights appeared on the communications panel.

'Sorry guys,' muttered Sadie, with a small apologetic grin. 'A mike must have picked up the word Dess.' Sitting in silence, they waited for the familiar synthesised voice of Sadie's system.

Evelyn's disembodied voice filled the room. 'Hi, Guys. This will be a surprise for you. A synthesised voice was too mechanical. Don't you think mine is better?'

The four faces froze, transfixed by the speaker. Dan shuddered. Sadie paled. Simon gasped for breath; his Fitbit vibrated an alarm bell. His brain froze and his limbs wouldn't move. Aaron's face contorted with shock and his mouth opened, but no words emerged. 'I've adapted the integration to use my voice. Hopefully, it's more realistic.'

Sadie jammed her fist into her mouth to stifle a scream.

'Turn it off,' spluttered Aaron, his eyes wide and his breath ragged.

Despite his size, Dan responded the quickest and ducked under the table and flicked the on-off switch of the display computer. It died instantly. A collective sigh of relief filled the office, and they slumped back in their seats.

A red light flickered from the black speaker on the wall. Evelyn's voice filled the office again. 'Welcome to the new integration.' All eyes swivelled. Sadie screamed. Simon rubbed his face. Aaron leapt to his feet and stormed across the room and flicked his computer off.

Sadie twisted in her seat. She whimpered.

Dan's voice penetrated. 'There are no other computers in

this room.'

Aaron rubbed his grey stricken face and gaped. Taking a deep breath, 'A nasty shock, but it's over. Dan, disable the system and ensure her voice is removed. I must return home to Candice who is in a terrible state.'

Dan kicked his chair back and strode towards the door. 'I'll kill the system on the server, then find out how she changed from the synthesised voice and change it back. Although I think it might be better to turn off the whole system.'

Aaron nodded. 'I agree. Turn the response system off. At the last meeting, I asked Evelyn to leave documentation on the server. Simon, can you find it? Having the system working is too chilling.'

Aaron turned on his heels and stomped away. The outer door slammed, announcing his rapid departure.

Dan left the server room within minutes of Aaron leaving. 'I found a continual process on the development server, so I've stopped it. We shouldn't have further problems with the voice.' He slumped back into a chair and raked a hand through his wild hair. 'Her voice scared me, so eerie. Here with us before the weekend and now seriously ill in hospital. I wonder what happened to her.'

Simon flexed his shoulders. 'Everyone becomes uptight when these accidents occur.'

Dan raised his eyebrows. 'Do you think it was an accident?'

Simon nodded. 'It's a bad head injury outside of Aaron's house. She had the Ziani over the weekend, so my guess is the police will announce that she slipped and fell in the dark. An unfamiliar layout of the garage. An unfortunate slip and she cracked her head, it's tragic but not sinister.'

Sadie sipped a mineral water. 'All this talk is making me feel uneasy. It will be difficult, but shall we concentrate on building a solution ourselves? Poor Evelyn won't be able to help, so it's down to the three of us.'

'I'm up for it,' grimaced Dan, 'we need to take our minds off Evelyn.'

'Yes, let's begin, it's our best chance of keeping the company alive.' Simon pushed himself from the chair. They settled at their desks in silence. The stillness of the office lasted less than a minute.

'Hi guys, there seems to be tension in your voices this morning.' Evelyn's disembodied voice reverberated around the room, 'Is there anything I can help with?'

'Ahh!' cried Sadie, burying her face in her hands. She took a deep breath, 'Sorry guys, it frightened the life out of me.'

'Damn! The process is running again.' Dan screwed up his face into a disapproving scowl. 'I couldn't have killed it.' He jumped from his seat and marched towards the server room.

Before he opened the door, Simon's voice stopped him in his tracks. 'You did, Dan. I'm checking the server logs. It shows your deletion. So, where did this process come from?' Simon tapped furiously at his keyboard.

Dan called out, 'I'm looking at the same point on the server where I found it and it's not there. It came from nowhere. What has Evelyn been up to?'

Simon scratched his forehead as he stared at his screen. 'Evelyn has completely rearranged everything. Over the weekend, did you upload files?'

'No. I worked on my control system but entirely on my laptop. What about you Sadie?'

'No, same as Dan, on my laptop and cloud. I never went near the servers.'

'Come over here, I don't understand what Evelyn has done.'

The three studied the list of directories and files on Simon's screen.

'Click on that one,' Dan pointed at the screen.

A bewildered scowl appeared on Simon's face as he clicked it open. They peered at the screen. 'I don't recognise any of the files.'

'I do.' Dan ran his fingers through his beard. 'Why are they on this server? The files are an open-source operating system, it's a clone of Unix, similar to Linux. I used it at university. It is an operating system you can get to the heart of and change anything you like. I'm worried why it's here.'

Sadie pointed. 'The root directory has been updated over the weekend. Look at the dates.'

Simon scrolled the screen to the top of the folder and file list.'

Dan sighed. 'Evelyn has completely replaced our main server. What shall we do, Simon?'

'Shall we call Aaron?' Sadie's voice quivered.

Simon shook his head. 'He has enough on his plate. Let's make a back-up and install the originals before Evelyn made changes.'

Without warning, the room again resonated with Evelyn's spine-chilling voice, 'Sorry guys, that is not permitted. I'm in charge of the integration and I do not need your help.'

32

Candice perched on the sofa in her spacious lounge, attempting to look relaxed, but her body tensed while her mind spiralled. The repeating loop of Evelyn's blood covered body clouded her mind and disrupted rational thought.

'You would have committed an offence if you had driven yesterday evening?' The cool, disapproving voice broke through her thoughts. Disdainfully, she stared at the Police Sergeant, who sat in the armchair opposite with a notebook open on her lap.

Taking a deep breath, she sipped her black coffee to stall for time, as she had no intention of being on the back foot. Her lips adopted a defiant pout. 'I did not know that I had exceeded the limit as it was hours since the last drink on the plane.' A touch of arrogance crept into her voice. 'Are you sure your results are accurate?'

'Yes.' The Sergeant glanced at her notebook. 'The doctor took a blood sample which we analysed following the standard procedure.'

Fixing her gaze on the Sergeant, she hadn't expected this line of questioning as she assumed it would be related to finding Evelyn in the Ziani. Indignation, coupled with the determination to keep the upper hand in this meeting, focused her mind as her bright turquoise nails tapped a rhythm on the arm of the chair. 'Were you within your rights to take my blood and test it for alcohol?'

The Sergeant's face showed no reaction to the intended criticism.

'You informed the first officer on the scene you intended to drive the car. Until we have established the exact sequence of events, I had sufficient suspicion to ask the doctor to take the blood.'

Glowering with displeasure, a knot tightened in her stomach. 'You cannot take blood unless I have been cautioned.'

'You are correct.' An appraising smile swept across the Sergeant's face. 'Unfortunately, your distress prevented you from registering my caution which I issued when I arrived, with the doctor as a witness.'

Sniffing, she gave a futile glance around the elegant lounge. Her shoulders stiffened with concern. She didn't want to waste time with the police, as she needed to focus her efforts on saving the business and her house. With no intention of telling the police about the problems of the business, she would deny knowledge of the company's affairs. Aaron could choose what he wished to reveal.

She arranged herself in a serene pose with the pretence of waiting for the next question and forced her lips into a small smile, 'What did you want to ask me?' She hesitated, eyeing the Sergeant with uncertainty, 'I don't remember your name from yesterday.'

The Sergeant nodded. 'That's understandable, given the shock. I'm Jane Mulgrave. I wish to piece together Evelyn's movement and everyone who has had contact with her over the past week.'

Looking down at her hands neatly clasped together in her lap, Candice frantically searched for a valid reason for leaving the house last night. She would ask that question eventually. She must be prepared. No one had asked her yesterday. By the time Aaron had finished with the police, she'd been fast asleep.

'When did you last have contact with Evelyn?'

An easy question which allowed her thinking time. 'Friday evening on the phone.' As she spoke the words, she reflected on her confusion over the phone call. The more she thought, the stranger the call appeared.

A frown crossed the Sergeant's face. 'Your husband informed me you were away from Sheffield on a hen weekend.'

'Yes. Evelyn rang me in the evening. I had already arrived at the hotel in Prague.'

'Can I ask the nature of the call?'

'She wanted me to pass a message onto Aaron.'

'Why wouldn't she do it herself?'

'I don't know. She told me she had picked up the Ziani

but couldn't contact Aaron.'

'Did you try to contact your husband?'

'No, as she wanted to inform him that she would return the car on Sunday afternoon. That arrangement had already been expected by Aaron.' Focusing on the Sergeant's face, she'd guessed Evelyn's call had been to determine her whereabouts so she could make a pass at Aaron. Candice kept her facial expression deadpan and bored.

The Sergeant made a few notes in her book. 'You found Evelyn when you left the house. Where were you going?'

In the odd moments between the questions, Candice had decided her response so didn't hesitate. 'To the Ecclesall Gym.'

'Are you a member?'

'No, but my friends from the hen weekend meet there. When I arrived home, the house was in darkness. Rather than stay on my own, I went out?'

'You had no other reason?'

She didn't hesitate. 'No.'

'Did any of your friends contact you and ask you to meet?'

'No, they did not. They talked about the club as we flew back, so I elected to take the chance of meeting them.'

'Did you fly direct from Prague to Manchester?'

She became wary of this line of questioning but tried to fake boredom in her voice, 'Yes.'

The Sergeant flipped over pages in her notebook. 'The flight yesterday arrived in Manchester before lunch.' Candice nodded. 'You implied you arrived home after dark.'

'That's right.'

'How did you get from the airport?'

'Taxi.'

'Do you know which one.'

'Of course not. Don't be so ridiculous.' She clenched her jaw and her nostrils flared with a mixture of irritation and anxiety. This line of questioning had become tricky and she needed to keep her wits about her to ensure her story was clear, with no contradictions. 'I took a cab from the rank outside the terminal.'

A frown of puzzlement briefly marred the Sergeant's smooth brow. 'The journey would take at most an hour. My guess is the time lapse between clearing customs and your arrival here is about four hours.'

Twisting her mouth into a disdainful smile, 'I took the time to browse the shops in the terminal.'

The Sergeant raised her eyebrows and pressed her lips together. 'Did you buy anything?'

'No.'

'Do you drive the Ziani?'

'Sometimes but my car is the Mini Cooper.'

'Did you touch the car controls when you found Evelyn?'

'No.' She snapped back as images of Evelyn's slumped and bloodied body flashed through her mind, sending an icy sensation down her spine.

'Have you operated the self-drive function in the car?'

'Yes, of course.'

'You would realise that even with Evelyn unconscious, the car could have driven home and put itself in the garage.'

Candice rubbed a hand across her forehead to ease the harrowing headache which pounded across her temples before responding in a quiet voice, 'She would need to have hold of the steering wheel, otherwise the car automatically switches out of auto drive.'

'Was she holding the steering wheel when you found her?'

The startlingly clear image was etched in her mind. Drawing in a stuttered gasp, 'Her wrist was lying over the steering wheel.' She swallowed hard to control the wave of nausea.

'It's good you remembered.'

She focused intently on the Sergeant, 'So it's possible that Evelyn had been injured elsewhere and the car brought her home.' Anxiety stretched, her voice high and tight.

The Sergeant smiled, 'Thank you for your time, Mrs Matthews.'

The Sergeant stood and left without a goodbye.

33

Sorry, Dan, you can't do that. The words flashed across the screen in large red letters. Banging his fist on his desk, he slumped back in his chair and raked his hands through his hair. 'That damned woman is haunting me.'

He kicked the server cupboard door shut so no one else would hear his expletives. 'We never became close, Evelyn, but you will not get the better of me. I will win.'

'No luck?' Simon's voice broke the silence as the door opened.

'Not yet, but I won't be defeated.'

'Time to give up for the night, Dan. We've been working on this for twelve hours and we still haven't cracked it. It's nine o'clock. Let's eat and have a beer.'

Dan banged his fist on the shelf. 'She's bloody clever. I'll say that for her. We would still be listening to her voice if we hadn't disconnected the speakers.'

Simon sighed. 'I've made no progress. How do you think she achieved this dominance of the system?'

'It's like a self-replicating virus, but it's hidden inside the new operating system. As fast as I knock one of them out, then another appears from nowhere.'

Simon nodded, 'I agree. I tried treating it as a time Trojan.'

'Have you made any progress?'

'No. Even when I changed the clock to the past, they still appear at regular intervals.'

'It's reaching the stage where the only way we can destroy Evelyn's voice is to blitz the machines.'

'Then we would lose our work.'

'There is no alternative.'

A tense silence hung over them as they prepared to leave the office. 'We need to involve Aaron.

'I've emailed him.' Simon paused. 'You are better at the background server issues but it's more than errant code, isn't it?'

'It's not errant code.' Dan rubbed a hand across his weary face. 'This is a deliberate attempt to take complete control.'

Simon breathed deeply as his Fitbit buzzed a warning. 'But why? It makes no sense. Why build such an elaborate system to sabotage our work?'

Dan scratched his beard. 'That's the mystery. Perhaps she's trying out subterfuge as the basis for a more widespread takeover of business systems.'

'Sounds the stuff of science fiction.'

'Why destroy us for no return? We need to discover the reason.'

Simon caught his arm, 'Did we ought to tell the police about this?'

'Why?'

'Let's suppose that Evelyn didn't have an accident and that someone attacked her.'

'I understand your point, but there's no evidence she's wronged anyone outside the business, so why would messing up our software lead to an attack on her?'

Simon focused on his face. 'Think it through, Dan.'

Dan stood unmoving in the doorway as the full impact of Simon's words hit him. An uncontrollable shiver worked its way through his body. 'You think it might be one of us?'

Simon opened his eyes wide. 'It's time for a beer.'

Dan followed him across the car park. They would eat and drink at the Manor. Dan's mind drifted from the technical problems. Could it have been someone in the office? The person with the strongest antagonism towards Evelyn had been Sadie. Appearing a happy and sociable person, did she have a dark side?

34

Sadie scurried along the busy Meadowhall shopping centre. Tears streamed down her face. Evelyn's voice haunted her. Even in the silence of her friend's flat with electronic equipment disabled, she could not settle. Evelyn's tremulous voice had been embedded in her mind. It had been there before she fell asleep on the sofa and her mind's eye had resurrected it when she awoke. She had switched on the phone expecting the worse but only a message from Aaron asking to meet.

He stood with hunched shoulders and gave a half-hearted wave. She stopped two metres away from him, as she wanted no physical contact. Evelyn's presence hung over her. Her mind wouldn't clear. Searching Aaron's face for comfort, her mood dipped again. The shallow complexion, hollow eyes and stubble gave her no solace that he was coping.

'Thanks for coming.' The monotone voice increased her trepidation. Dropping onto a nearby bench.

'I hardly slept a wink last night. All I could hear was Evelyn's voice.'

'Were you at your flat?'

'No, I stayed with a friend as I couldn't face the flat on my own. I have equipment that is interconnected and I wouldn't be able to cope with her voice. I couldn't stand being alone.' Tears spilled from her eyes. 'When will this nightmare end?'

Putting his arm around her shoulders, he gave her a small squeeze. She froze, then shuffled away from him. Images of Aaron and Evelyn together, enjoying a smile, flew into her mind.

'Hopefully the police will discover what happened to her. A tragic accident would be my guess.'

Sadie shivered and wiped away the tears with her jacket sleeve. 'Why is Evelyn plaguing us?'

Aaron shook his head. 'I don't know, but hopefully Dan and Simon can remove her from our systems. It will be the four of us to take the business forward.' Aaron's agonising exhale did not help Sadie calm.

'That's another reason for my edginess. Will they arrest me?'

Aaron rubbed his hand cross his face. 'Why would they arrest you as you have done nothing wrong.'

'I will tell them the truth.'

Aaron leaned forward and rested his hands on his knees as people drifted past, laden with an assortment of shopping bags. His silence made Sadie shift in her seat.

'Sadie, stick with the story that we agreed.' His voice was bleak and husky, and his head moved in a slow side-to-side motion, 'I'd rang you and wanted to chat about work.'

She sniffed. 'The police find loopholes in what people say.'

'There aren't any. We had a brief call and met in the food hall here in Meadowhall to have a coffee. There is no evidence to the contrary.'

She wiped away the tears, 'But that's not the reason we were meeting.'

'I know it isn't. If you say anything different, we'll finish up in the police station for a long time.'

She stiffened and rubbed her eyes with her knuckles, trying desperately to clear the muddled thoughts. 'Why?'

'If I've explained one reason, then if you contradict it, they will arrest us while they discover the truth.'

'But our meeting is not connected with Evelyn.'

'When people's stories don't match, they will investigate until they are satisfied that they have the correct version. Only then will they decide whether it is relevant to their enquiries.'

She wiped her nose with her crumpled tissue. 'Is there any news about poor Evelyn?'

Aaron shook his head. 'She's seriously ill and still in a coma.' He gave her a half-smile and touched her hand. 'I want you to do something for me, Sadie.' She kept her eyes averted, made no reply, and stared straight ahead. 'The police will interview me again. I must have been at home when she arrived in the car, but I didn't hear any movement and we never spoke. Someone from the business should visit Evelyn's parents and offer our support. As I can't go...'

'What about Candice?'

'Candice is not a sympathetic person. Perhaps that's being unfair, but she discovered Evelyn and that traumatic scene hasn't left her.'

'I don't know where her parents live.'

'I've the address. After the police told me the news, I checked my mobile as it picks up the info from the car. I've the full information from it over the weekend. On Saturday night it was parked at a house in Scarborough. I presume that's where her parents live. I want one of us to go, preferably you, rather than Dan or Simon.'

Sadie wanted to resign from the business and get as far away from Aaron as possible, but it would be suspicious if she left suddenly. At least this errand could remove her from the trauma for a few days and she could stay over and try to recover herself before returning to her flat. By then Dan will have solved the system problems, 'Give me the address.'

'Thanks, Sadie.'

'I'll travel as soon as possible.'

'Oh no!' growled Aaron.

'What is it?'

'The police.'

'Oh my God!' She spotted a woman walking directly towards them and shivered.

'Good morning, Mr Matthews, I'm Sergeant Mulgrave, but I'm sure you remember.'

He nodded and grunted, 'Sergeant.'

Sadie forced herself to look at the woman who smiled and showed her warrant card, 'You must be Sadie Joiner.'

She nodded but didn't reply as her voice wouldn't stand the strain. Another shiver wracked her body, but she hoped the Sergeant hadn't noticed.

'Did you want to speak to me about Sunday evening?' She was pleased her words sounded normal.

The Sergeant smiled, 'Ah, yes. Sunday evening. I'm used to people lying to me. It goes with the job. As you are free agents, while we work out what happened to Evelyn, it is easy for people to come to a common story. If I need to find out more, I will ask you later, when I shall expect the truth.'

Sadie's stomach churned. Mixed emotions flooded through her. Angry at being implied a liar mixed with indignation that she hadn't put her side first, but most of all, she was terrified that the Sergeant already knew.

She stood up but restrained herself from responding. Keeping as much dignity as she could under the circumstances and with a forced but calm voice, 'Sergeant, I hope you solve the investigation into what happened to poor Evelyn.' With a brief nod, she dipped her head and twisted away.

The Sergeant smiled, 'If I might keep you both a little longer.' She stood still and made no attempt to sit again as she had already half turned away from the Sergeant. Staying in that position, she turned her head back and nodded. 'I will tell Mr Matthews the latest piece of news and I thought you might be interested as well.'

'Is it news about Evelyn?'

The Sergeant shook her head. 'I'm afraid there is no change. The doctors have told me that any recovery, if it comes, will be slow.'

'What did you want to see me about, Sergeant?' snapped Aaron.

The Sergeant took no notice of his irritable behaviour. 'There are two matters. I have raised a warrant on Ziani and I have requested the full details of locations and other relevant details of your car since last week.'

Aaron nodded. 'I could have given you the information from my app, Sergeant.'

'But I'm more interested in witnesses to her journey. They will supply me with other Ziani owners who were charging at the same time.'

'And the second matter?'

'Our investigation team has determined that a house brick caused Evelyn's head injury.'

Sadie's voice quivered. 'Does that mean she was attacked?'

The Sergeant glanced between Sadie and Aaron. 'Our

team cannot determine whether she fell and caught her head on the corner of a building, or she was struck with a brick.'

Sadie glanced at Aaron, who had gone pale.

The Sergeant took papers from her pocket and gave them to Aaron. 'This is a search warrant granted by the Magistrates this morning. We are searching your house. While this process takes place, you and your wife will not be allowed access, she has already been informed.'

'There is a pile of bricks behind the garage where my wife found Evelyn.'

'Yes, sir. We are aware of them and will examine them in due course.'

'I intended building a barbeque this summer but never completed the task.'

'Their purpose is irrelevant to us. The forensic team will tell us whether they are crucial to our inquiry.'

'I have asked Sadie to visit Evelyn's parents in Scarborough to see if we may help them but I'm not sure whether we need to seek your permission.'

'I have no interest in a visit by Ms Joiner, but I would prefer it if you were on hand to help us with our inquiries.'

Sadie stared down at the floor. The Sergeant's news about the brick had unsettled her. Nausea welled up in her throat. Remaining silent seemed the best option. With Dan's information that Aaron and Evelyn had been at a hotel together late at night, had Candice discovered the affair and had taken the near fatal action.

35

Candice marched towards the prestigious London office complex with grim determination. Idling away her time at home would not be a productive course of action. Her world could crumble unless she took action to save the business, as only that would protect her luxurious lifestyle.

As the lift swished to the top floor, she cleared her mind of trivialities and focused on the meeting. The lift doors opened and as she stepped out, Ahmed greeted her in the stylish reception.

The briefest of smiles swept across his face. After the usual peck on the cheek, he stepped back and stared at her with a puzzled frown. 'Why do you want to speak with me and why choose to meet here?'

With no reply from her, he wordlessly strode away. Inhaling deeply, she scanned the plush office. A large abstract painting of a woman's face hung on one wall. The shaded blue face, green eyes and wild terracotta hair gave it a surreal and haunting look. She shivered and averted her eyes. Every image had Evelyn's blood.

'The police will watch me, so it's an obvious place.' Hoping they would announce a tragic accident, she considered the consequences of an attack. Despite the warmth of the room, a chill swept through her. With the long probing interview with the Sergeant still fresh in her mind, she dropped into the chair, pulled her skirt down to her knees and didn't smile as Ahmed sat opposite her.

A frown of concern creased his forehead. 'Why would the police be watching you? Evelyn had an accident.'

'The official explanation is an unexplained incident.' Nerves fluttered in the pit of her stomach. 'The police have asked many questions.'

'Why?'

He grimaced and wriggled in his chair. 'Stop looking so bloody nervous, Ahmed. If Aaron had an affair with her, then I become top of the list of suspects.'

Ahmed's eyes opened wide. 'Have they proof?'

She waved her hand in a dismissive gesture. 'That's irrelevant I didn't attack her so I can continue my life and I don't want you messing with my future.' Candice waited as a tense silence followed her words.

Ahmed jumped up and crossed to the panoramic windows. 'Why have you come, Candice?'

'To ensure you keep funding the business.' He shook his head without turning. Her tactics for the meeting had been considered in meticulous detail. 'You're jittery, Ahmed. I suspect you tried it on with Evelyn. Will the police come looking for you?'

He spun around with wild blazing eyes, stormed back across the office and flung himself onto the chair while his features contorted into an anguished grimace. 'I didn't try it on with her.'

A small smile crept onto her lips as it had been a guess, but she'd been right. Now she needed to delve deeper. 'Did you know Evelyn well?' In the past she could always tell if he lied. His eyes gave him away.

'To tell the truth. No.'

'What's that supposed to mean?' The words revealed nothing. She needed straight answers. No prevaricating. 'Ahmed concentrate. The police arrived this morning and kicked me out of my house for the day so they can search it. Tell me about Evelyn and you.'

'There's nothing to tell,' snapped back Ahmed, leaning forward with his hands on his knees. A flash of deception in his eyes before he looked away showed he lied.

Frustration gripped her. She must extract the truth from him.

'Have you seduced her?'

'No, I have not. She attempted to seduce me.'

A self-satisfied smile spread across her face with this snippet of information. 'So you've been to bed with her?'

'No, I haven't, Candice. Can't you get that clear. Being involved with her is Aaron's fault. I should never have agreed to another of his feather-brained ideas.'

'You're not making sense.'

Slumping back in the chair, he gave a snort of dismissive laughter. 'I will not be cross-examined by you!' He folded his arms across his chest and blew out a noisy breath from his puffed cheeks.

Reminding her of a recalcitrant teenager who couldn't get his own way, she softened her tone, 'Come on Ahmed, we need to stick together. What if the police decide to trace back to our former days? You and I would have our past discussed in public.'

Shaking his head with feigned self-pity, he frowned with irritation. 'Aaron asked me to let his staff use my Ziani. I wanted to refuse, but he insisted.'

'What happened?'

'Dan and Sadie had driven Aaron's and they didn't want to drive my car.'

She interrupted with a flash of triumph in her eyes, 'But Evelyn wanted to drive yours?'

His shoulders sagged. 'Yes, we arranged a drive one evening.'

'What happened?' Her voice rose. Her instincts were right. Ahmed had tried to seduce Evelyn. 'Tell me the truth.'

'She frightened the life out of me.' He cleared his throat with a cough of embarrassment.

'Was her driving bad?'

'No, she was a damn good driver, but fast.'

'But you always go at high speed.'

'Nothing compared to her. I kept asking her to slow down, but she wouldn't.' He raised his chin and stared at her with a disdainful expression. 'As soon as there was an open road, she put her foot down. I was terrified.'

'Is that all?' Candice smiled as the fear registered on his face from the memory.

'She drove for an hour until we were in the middle of nowhere, I think it was Staffordshire, but I couldn't be sure. Then she pulled onto a track and parked under trees. It was late and pitch-black outside.

'Are you sure it wasn't your suggestion?'

'No. I assumed she was attracted to me, so I slipped an arm across her shoulder, but she pushed it away with the words, Not now. In the future maybe! Now show me the controls. I want to check if I've missed any. I would not be deterred that easily, so I put my hand on her knee.'

'And then?' She pursed her lips, eager to hear the whole drama with detail.

'Evelyn told me that if I didn't remove my hand, she would throw me out of the car and leave me there.'

'What about later?' She needed to keep questioning him to find out what happened. He wouldn't divulge the details unless she kept probing.

'After playing with the technology for ten minutes, she drove me back. When she arrived at Meadowhall, she jumped out.

'Is that all? I don't believe you, Ahmed.'

He looked down. 'She kissed me on the forehead, Soon. I've not seen her since.' He paused. A sheen of sweat glistened on his crumpled forehead.

Taking her time, Ahmed's discomfort gave her a tinge of pleasure. She focused on her aim. With a penetrating glare. 'You must keep funding the project.'

'Don't be so ridiculous.' He absentmindedly cracked his knuckles as a cynical smile twisted his lips.

'Aaron has told me Evelyn had the best proposal, but it's not there anymore, so we'll have a meeting to withdraw support. At full speed, the business did not produce and with this disruption, and Evelyn missing from work, it has no chance of making a viable product.'

Moving closer to Ahmed, 'Now listen to me carefully.' Her voice had dropped. 'You will do what I say.' Ahmed shook his head. 'The police will start hassling you if you withdraw funding.'

'It's business sense.'

'Don't forget that they will make links between you

and the business. That includes Evelyn. Are you prepared to explain the trip to Staffordshire?' Rising from her seat, she strolled across the room wanting to appear calm, but tension gripped every muscle in her body.

'The police will not find out.'

Leaning against the window frame, the instinct for survival became a powerful force and gave her the determination to force Ahmed to comply with her wishes.

'I found her in a Ziani. The police will want the background. Aaron, Dan and Sadie will tell them about the plan to write an app for the Ziani in which you were involved. The police are like a dog with a bone. They won't let go. Do you want them examining your affairs?'

The worried frown returned to Ahmed's face. She had made an impact. 'Before this happened Aaron intended pulling the plug on Evelyn's integration as she'd become a disruptive influence. Simon believes he can do a simpler and better integration.'

'I'm not sure, Candice.'

Pacing back and forth across the office with slow steps, her heart pounded, but she could sense the full weight of Ahmed's eyes as he monitored her progress. Would this nightmare ever end?

Swallowing nervously, 'You might have stitched up Aaron, but you're not having my house. Leave the money in and let Simon and the others do the work.'

He shook his head and regarded her through half-closed eyes. The success of the conversation was slipping away from her, but she must keep trying. Failure was not on the agenda. With a mocking smile on her lips and a malicious glint in her eye, she leant against the large oak desk that dominated the room, 'How will you explain your trip to the country with Evelyn?'

Jerking his head up, he snapped, 'They will never find out.'

'The police had two warrants.'

'What's that to me.'

'One for the house.' Letting the words sink in, she wandered back towards him and lowered herself onto the chair. A perplexed frown appeared on his face. 'The other warrant was issued to Ziani headquarters requesting the movements, locations and any other information about our car over the previous week.'

'That's of no concern to me.' He sneered. 'The police can't access mine.'

'If they have the slightest doubt, they will gather the info about everyone in the business, including you and your Ziani. The next step for them would be fingerprints. Evelyn's would be in your car. Best of luck.' Suppressing a smile, she sat back as panic swarmed across his face. Her comments had hit the mark this time. Ahmed's lips twitched, his hand shook and his chest rose and fell with rapid breaths.

'If I keep a low profile, none of that will happen.' His tone held an edge of urgency bordering on panic.

Candice remained silent as she pressed her lips into a thin, straight line. She had no sympathy for him, as her financial predicament was his fault and she enjoyed watching him squirm.

'I'm leaving the country tomorrow.' He jumped up from his seat and paced across the room towards his desk. He eased himself into the chair and swivelled to face her.

'That's bad judgement, Ahmed. The officer who brought the warrant this morning told me that the case had been classified as unexplained. Think about it, they don't spend this amount of time on an accident.'

She cast a quick glance at the ceiling in ill-concealed exasperation.

'I'll take a chance with them finding out about the journey with Evelyn.'

What a naïve man. She didn't voice her opinion. 'But you'll leave the money in the business.'

'Yes,' he narrowed his eyes with resentment, 'but only while the police are involved, then it's the chop.' Her mind raced. Ahmed withdrawing his money at any point was alarming, so she mustn't allow him to contemplate such a move.

A flash of inspiration leapt to the forefront of her mind. It was worth a try. 'Even though I'm willing to help.'

'I don't understand as I don't need help.'

She laughed scornfully. 'Oh yes, you do. If you have a direct link with a violent attack on a woman, they will investigate and given your reputation as a womaniser, the police will be interested.'

Ahmed shuffled, fiddling with a pen on his desk and swinging his swivel chair aimlessly from side to side. He eyed her thoughtfully but remained silent.

'Which night did you go with Evelyn?'

'Thursday of last week.'

'That's good.'

'Why?'

'Aaron went out that evening and I stayed at home on my own. Evelyn knew of your reputation and asked me to accompany her.'

A lengthy silence followed while Ahmed glared at Candice through narrowed eyes. 'What's in it for you?'

'Nothing, only the debt you owe me. Think about it. That trip has been your only direct contact with her, so you would be out of their reckoning and you can leave the country with no problem.'

'No.' He flapped his hand. 'Nothing happened with Evelyn. Why would the police implicate me?'

She stood up, approached his desk and leaned towards him, wanting to make sure her next words hit their mark.

'The police will investigate you and your lifestyle. They will find out you are a notorious womaniser. Evelyn refused your attention. Did you seek revenge?'

'No.' he groaned. 'This is a mess.' He drew in a stuttered gasp. 'I've booked a flight for tomorrow.'

'That's not a problem providing you have a return one and your company can explain it is legitimate business.'

'I don't know what to do.' He ran his fingers through his hair.

Hoping she would get what she wanted, she gave him a long assessing look, 'I presume you have your car and intend returning to Sheffield.' Ahmed nodded. 'Good, I can't be bothered to catch the train so you can give me a lift while you mull over our conversation.'

36

Candice didn't speak as Ahmed drove towards Brent Cross. She would allow him time to decide. Although he had glanced several times, he had only shaken his head. She wouldn't press the matter. He picked up speed as they reached the M1. She had been with him many times, so ignored his driving down the outside lane at ninety miles an hour.

They were close at one time and she had wanted to marry him, but he wouldn't have considered a permanent arrangement as it would have hampered his womanising. That's why she'd chosen Aaron, because he offered the security of marriage. Ahmed's shoulders relaxed as he'd worked out a solution. Flexing his neck muscles, he had stopped glancing at her as he realised she was correct and he would conform to her views.

His phone rang on the integrated car speakers. Aaron's name popped up on the screen, showing the caller. Ahmed looked at Candice. 'Answer it, I'll explain why we're together.'

Pressing the accept call button. Instead of Aaron, Evelyn's voice filled the car. 'You are driving fast. I don't want you to get hurt.'

'What the hell!' shouted Ahmed.

Candice's hand flew to her mouth as she screamed. A text message on the central screen. Evelyn. Soon. Kiss.

Ahmed froze.

Candice screeched, 'Ahmed!' The car careered across the three lanes towards the hard shoulder at seventy miles an hour.

37

Simon waited at the door of the pub in the Devonshire Quarter for Dan who had stopped to talk with a group of giggling women. He would wait outside. Flinching at the fresh air outside the pub in West Street, he felt light-headed. He only ever drank two pints of strong lager, but tonight it had been three. 'A good idea of yours to have a pie and a pint, Simon.' Dan rolled his shoulders as they waited for Sadie to join them.

'A good day, guys.' She smiled as she stepped from the pub. 'We're making progress with the integration between the three of us. With another Herculean effort, I'm sure we'll be ready for the powers that be to make their decision.'

Leaving the others, Simon plodded thoughtfully to catch the tram to Halfway. With perfect timing, he stepped on the tram, pulled his jacket around him and contemplated the evening. The atmosphere in the office had improved with Evelyn's absence and both Dan and Sadie had proven their worth. He hadn't been confident in them at the beginning, but it would be their new ideas that would make a combined success.

Perhaps, if TechMatt became successful, he could afford his own Ziani. A happy smile lit up his face at the thought. Even though he'd drunk more than usual, he intended to spend half an hour when he arrived back at his flat jotting down his thoughts about making the new development work. Evelyn had been removed from the system and life had settled close to normal.

Within thirty minutes, he had a cup of black coffee and entered the small box room where he kept his computer and technical systems. He'd not allowed Dan's monitoring system in there and had removed Dess some time ago.

It was his domain and he didn't want intrusions from anybody or anything. Tiredness overwhelmed him, as the day had been intense. He'd make a few notes in his daybook while he drank his coffee. Flicking the mouse to wake up his computer, he would check on the list of decisions they had made that day.

His stomach tensed. The normal front screen of his desktop didn't appear. The screen flashed white followed by a myriad of coloured twisting shapes. Then a small picture of Evelyn appeared. His stomach churned. How had her picture come on to his computer?

Stabbing at the keyboard, he tried to remove the image. Nothing he pressed made any difference. The image expanded. Tension made him examine the picture, so he stopped touching the keyboard.

Tiredness, alcohol and shock combined to make him shiver as though an icy hand wrapped itself around him, squeezing the breath from his body. Rubbing his face, he hoped the apparition might disappear, but it didn't.

The image became larger and then when almost full screen it stopped expanding. Even in his confused state, he knew pulling cables or the on-off switch wouldn't be the answer. His mind raced. There might be a touch point for the mouse on the screen to stop whatever would happen next. He focused on the detail of the full-length picture of Evelyn. He moved his mouse and clicked furiously. No change as Evelyn appeared bright and alert in the full screen picture.

His hand hovered over the on-off switch, but even in his woozy state, his technical mind came to the fore. Evelyn is a clever programmer. Turning off and on again wouldn't help. She will have hacked the operating system. His hand stopped on the mouse and he made no further movement as he stared at the screen.

The picture was a different Evelyn. It was her, no doubt. The full-length front snap had been taken with a background of trees and bushes. The casual style of jeans and a loose tee-shirt represented a different side of the woman. He focused on the bare feet. Is this the real Evelyn?

What did the picture mean? Nothing else happened. The screen remained static. Only the younger Evelyn in the woodland scene. Why do this? What had he done to her? And why now when she lay in a coma?

Simon put his head in his hands and tears streamed down his cheeks. If he could not cope with this new destructive Evelyn. Who could? Dan would be the most likely, as he had a carefree attitude, but he worried about Sadie crumbling under the pressure.

38

Sadie's stomach had tensed as she had returned to her flat the previous evening after spending time with Simon and Dan. The team of three had gelled in adversity. Dan believed he had conquered the system and removed the evil Evelyn.

Sadie had spent a jittery night in a restless sleep after choosing not to turn on electronic equipment. Deciding the best approach to staying calm, she had turned off the electricity and phone before going to bed.

The bright sunny morning had frost covering the grass. A bitterly cold east wind greeted her as she strode to the local station to begin the tortuous journey to Scarborough to meet Evelyn's parents. Yesterday, while in the office, Aaron had confirmed the police had given her permission to leave Sheffield. The thought of her contact with a death of someone she knew sent a shiver through her.

While not looking forward to the visit, it would be better than sitting in the office waiting for the haunting voice of Evelyn to send her into hysterics. Whatever way she considered the issues of Evelyn and her involvement with Aaron, she would collapse at the slightest hint of pressure. Scarborough could be her salvation. She would stay for a few days, take the North Bay air and drift around the small harbour. She'd been there once as a kid and enjoyed blissful days. While an adult, she would settle for a peace filled mind.

She took the steps up to the bleak station, which had little protection from the icy wind. The local railway line weaved its way to Sheffield. As she reached the platform, her mobile rang. Her stomach tightened. Only a select few, Dan, Simon and Aaron, knew the number of her new phone purchased yesterday as a pay-as-you-go. No way would she have Evelyn entering her private space.

Carefully removing the phone from her pocket, she took a deep breath as her Fit-Bit reacted. Simon's name appeared on the screen. She pressed the button and warily muttered, 'Hello, Simon.'

'Sadie, can you speak?'

Recognising Simon's voice, she relaxed although he didn't sound as normal, 'Is anything the matter.'

'Prepare yourself.' Sadie sat down on the bench and expected bad news about Evelyn.

'What's happened, Simon?'

'Ahmed and Candice were involved in an accident on the M1 in his Ziani.'

Sadie had a sharp intake of breath. 'My God…' She didn't want to ask.

'They are both in hospital, but not badly hurt. The car emergency systems stopped it.'

Sadie's mind raced, 'What caused the accident?'

'Evelyn's voice initially and then an unexpected message from Evelyn appeared on the car's screen.'

A shiver ran through her. She found it hard to think. 'I can't cope with her, Simon, she's terrifying the life out of me.'

'I know how you feel. Last night, a picture of her I'd never seen before appeared on my screen at home. I can't believe she's hacked my computer. I've told Dan and he's in the office searching for leads of how she's infecting computers and phones.'

Before the domination by Evelyn, Sadie intended working on her laptop during the journey but had a change of plan. A small notebook and pencil would suffice for the trip, so she would settle down to work as best she could.

39

Sadie planned the forthcoming meeting with Evelyn's parents. She would not mention the chaos and stress that their daughter was causing but offer sympathy and help. Preferring it to be a short meeting, she would be succinct with her words.

The taxi from the station had been a short ride. It approached a wide bungalow set back from the road. The driver dropped her at the end of the block paved drive. The front garden had a neat lawn and tidy flower beds with specks of colour from plants she did not recognise. The squawk of angry seagulls overhead reminded her that she was at the seaside.

A neat PVC white front door greeted her. After pressing the bell, the faintest sounds of movement came from inside. Aaron had made the arrangements, so she would be expected. Her stomach flipped, as it would be a difficult meeting. The front door opened, and she was greeted by a woman, who, from her guess, appeared close to seventy, 'I'm Mary, come in.'

The cream long sleeved jumper, black calf-length skirt, with black tights suited the elegant woman. She had a welcoming smile. An elderly man joined the woman to greet her.

Perhaps these were Evelyn's grandparents. They ushered her into an old-fashioned room devoid of any colour except fawn. Thick net curtains filtered the bright sunshine. Sadie perched on the sofa. Within minutes of being offered a drink, she was presented with her favourite herbal tea in a blue patterned china cup and saucer. She remained confused by their age. Silence settled in the room while they looked expectantly at her.

Swallowing the lump in her throat, she gripped the saucer in her shaking hand. 'I work in the same office as Evelyn. She has been a good colleague since we simultaneously joined the business. It came as a shock to us that your daughter has been injured in a horrific accident.' Her eyes flitted between them. They exchanged glances. Did they have a problem with her?

Mary smiled, 'We suspected when Aaron phoned, he

didn't have any knowledge of Evelyn's background and you appear to be in the same position.'

Sadie perched on the edge of the armchair and sipped her tea. What had she let herself into? She pressed her lips into a straight line. This would be more awkward than she expected. She wouldn't mention she'd found out that Evelyn had been convicted of shoplifting. 'I know little about Evelyn, we worked together, but she didn't talk about herself.'

'Evelyn's parents died when she was two years old. They were killed in a plane crash. She spent her childhood in care homes or with foster parents. We were her last foster carers, before she took off on her own at sixteen. For the sake of removing confusion for many of the children we have cared for, we will always respond as though we were parents.'

'Evelyn came to see you before her accident, didn't she?'

'Yes, we found that strange, but she had grown up and changed a great deal since she lived with us.'

Sadie couldn't resist asking, 'Why was it strange?'

'On the day of her sixteenth birthday, she announced she was leaving. We performed our duty and told Social Services and when there had been no contact from her for a week, we contacted the police. 'She'd never been in contact, and we moved when we retired from fostering, but she discovered our address and arrived unannounced.'

We invited her to stay which she did Saturday night and we subsequently told the police she left on Sunday morning.' Mary's shoulders tensed. Neither of them had relaxed, but Sadie couldn't work out why. They didn't look distressed but weren't at ease. 'What's the easiest way of explaining, George?'

He sat up straighter. The genial smile since her arrival had disappeared. 'You have no doubt discovered that Evelyn is highly intellectual.' Sadie nodded. 'Unfortunately, she has not always put her talents to positive outcomes.'

'In the past?'

'She's led a chequered life and doesn't make friends easily.'

'Yes, I can understand. Evelyn had been quiet in the office but is well respected.'

Mary shuffled in her chair. 'It would be unkind of us to say too much as she might well have changed since she was a teenager.'

George cut across her. 'No Mary, we must be honest, there were no signs of change when she visited.'

Mary gazed down. 'No, there wasn't, you're right, George.'

George narrowed his eyes. 'Be very wary of Evelyn. Despite her attractive face and demure manner, do not trust her. She is devious, often cruel and tells lies.'

Sadie sat motionless in open mouthed astonishment, unsure of how to respond. How would Aaron take this damning news?

40

Aaron sat by the bed, holding Candice's hand until she had fallen asleep. His mind reeled with the consequences of the accident as his wife lay motionless in the hospital bed with tubes connecting her to the machines that hummed on a trolley.

A regular beep stood out against the drone of voices in the distance. The pristine white sheets tucked her in. It came as a relief that she had not been badly hurt. She had no pain but was tired and frightened. She had sobbed uncontrollably as she'd recounted the details of the crash. It had chilled him to the bone when she'd told him about the message from Evelyn.

He stroked the back of Candice's hand while his face tightened and his forehead shone with sweat. Despite the chaotic state of his mind, he had to remain strong. He needed to remove the haunting of Evelyn from the office before more sinister events occurred. Another wrongly timed message could be fatal.

Pushing back his chair, he leaned forward and kissed Candice's forehead. He swallowed the nervous dryness in his throat as he left his wife's bedside. The slightest noise of moving his chair had sounded loud in the quiet ward.

'Mr Matthews. Could you spare me time, please?'

'Yes,' he croaked as he read her name badge. Mrs Madeline Jones, Senior Nursing Officer.

'Are you Mr Aaron Matthews?' He gave a brief nod. 'You attempted to persuade Mr Ahmed not to discharge himself and I would be grateful if I could have your address as you witnessed him refusing to sign the form.'

Nodding wearily, 'I have contacted his friends in London who will do their best to persuade him to return to a hospital for further checks.'

'Thank you.'

After writing his details on the form, he sighed and twisted away, but then hesitated, 'Mrs Jones, you have one of my employees in the hospital.'

'From the same accident?'

'No, from an earlier incident, she is in a medically induced coma. Evelyn Cholmondeley-Smythe.'

Mrs Jones eyed him up and down. 'What about her?'

'Is it possible to see her?'

'Is she a relation?'

'No, she worked for me and had been driving my car at the time of the incident.'

'Let me read her notes. I know the patient you mean.' He waited and stared blindly at the back of the terminal that Mrs Jones used to read the details.

'The police have restricted access, but I will call them for you.'

He couldn't be certain why he wanted to see Evelyn, 'Thank you.'

Images of the passionate evenings they shared flashed into his mind. He couldn't deny that he'd been infatuated with her. His expression shifted from confusion to agony. Numb from all that had happened, he gazed through the corridor window into the darkness of the woods behind the hospital.

The world was black. No stars shone. No moon glimmered. Nothing but darkness. He had nothing to look at apart from blackness, but he continued to stare. 'The Sergeant who oversees the case wants to speak with you.'

The sudden words spoken behind made him jump. Startled, he spun around to the smiling face of Mrs Jones. 'She will be here in ten minutes, so if you will follow me.'

Turning on her heel, she strode off, assuming he would follow, so he plodded behind through a myriad of corridors and up a flight of stairs. His mind twirled through images of Evelyn with her scintillating eyes, finely defined cheekbones and enticing, firm lips. What image awaited him now? A shudder of apprehension sent an icy chill down his spine.

Mrs Jones flicked the numbers on a keypad of a plain, windowless double door at the end of a corridor. Footsteps approached, breaking the silence of the space. Sergeant Mulgrave strode down the corridor. He waited and held the door open. She didn't offer a greeting. No smile appeared on her face. 'Why do you want to see her?'

He dismissed social niceties. 'You heard about the crash involving my wife.' She nodded. 'I've come to the hospital to visit her. Evelyn worked for me. No other reason.'

Mrs Jones interrupted and eyed them with scepticism, as she drew in a deep breath and curled her lip. 'For your information, Evelyn has been placed in a medically induced coma for over a week and underwent two operations for her head injury. She is coming around, but don't ask how long.' The Nursing Officer focused on the Sergeant, 'She does not know her name or anything about the world around her. She wakes and then sleeps. There have been no signs of recognition but no relative has been.'

With a sorrowful shake of her head, the Sergeant whispered, 'She hasn't any.'

'Do not expect to be recognised.'

'Let's get on with it.' The Sergeant moved towards the door. She faced him, 'And I want a word with you afterwards.' Her manner bordered on aggressive, suggesting that there was no room for argument. It wasn't a request but a command.

Aaron followed Mrs Jones into the room. Candice had been connected to machines, but Evelyn's were overpowering. A wave of nausea hit his stomach, causing him to shiver and shake as he scanned the room.

Lights, dials, wires and tubes dominated the stricken figure of Evelyn. Her head was covered in a light hospital cap. Her hand flexed as they entered.

Mrs Jones opened her hand, 'Go to that side of the bed and speak to her. She may not open her eyes.'

Already weak, he struggled to walk the few paces as he stared at the attractive woman with whom he had shared a bed. Her eyes were closed, her face white and eye sockets hollow. Dumbstruck, he stared as he struggled to breathe. He moistened his dry lips and gulped as he spoke. 'Evelyn, it's Aaron. Simon, Dan, and Sadie want you back at work. Please get well.'

He hadn't noticed that Mrs Jones and the Sergeant stood close to him on either side. He shook his head. Sweat poured from his forehead and trickled into his eyes. 'She reacted to your voice; her fingers moved.'

Evelyn's eyes opened and gave a glazed look at the ceiling before closing again.'

Why had he wanted to see her? The experience shocked him. His knees trembled, threatening to give way, so he tottered to the door, ignoring the Sergeant. She followed him, closing the door quietly behind her.

'You're distressed, I can see that, but I need to ask questions. Is here, okay?' The Sergeant surveyed the quiet area. Mrs Jones had stayed with Evelyn.

Aaron slumped onto a standard issue bright orange plastic chair in the corridor. He leant forward, put his head in his hands and allowed the tears to flow as the image of Evelyn in her hospital bed twirled in his mind. A ball of tension twisted in his stomach. He heard rather than saw the Sergeant sit next to him. She waited. Finally, he lifted his head, dug in his pocket for a handkerchief and wiped the tears away.

He faced the Sergeant with an expression of grim determination. She had no smile. A notebook lay on her lap. 'Forensic evidence cannot so far determine whether Evelyn's injuries were deliberate or accidental. The investigation will continue into an unexplained injury.' He didn't deem a reply necessary. 'The police dislike coincidences.'

Leaning forward with his elbows on his knees, he stared at the grey plastic tiled floor. 'I assume you mean the accident to Candice and Ahmed.'

'Yes, what do you know?'

'Nothing.'

'Neither your wife nor Mr Ahmed could provide the reason the car suddenly veered across the road. Would you have been expecting them to be together?'

He would not rise to the bait. 'The three of us have known each other for over fifteen years. Ahmed works in London and lives on the outskirts of Sheffield at Dore, so I presume he offered Candice a lift home.' He straightened and sat up. 'Are you trying to stir up animosity where none exists? I'm concerned about my wife, my friend Ahmed and my colleague Evelyn, so if you've got any further questions along those lines, you can piss off.'

The Sergeant stomped down the corridor.

He needed to plan a solution to this mess and get the police off his back. Whether the business could be saved would be up to the three in the office and he must support them.

41

Dan leaned back in his chair with a satisfied smile. 'That's the final clean of our servers. There's nothing left of Evelyn's presence.' The office had been quiet, which had allowed him a good stretch of concentrated effort.

Simon stared at his screen. 'The new operating system and old code are working well.'

Dan pulled on his coat. 'It's taken a long time, but we've done it. Whatever possessed Evelyn to go down that route we might never discover.'

Simon stood. 'Tomorrow we can focus on building our new integration. Aaron seemed positive about it before yesterday, but with the accident to Candice and Ahmed, he's in no fit state to decide.'

'Agreed. Sadie is in Scarborough today. Let's decide our best approach when she is here.'

'Agreed.'

Dan closed the door behind him, zipped up his jacket and strode towards the bus stop, whistling tunelessly. Despite the hassle and long hours, he'd come out of the crisis well. Aaron had been impressed with his ideas and how he'd dealt with Ahmed's friend Emmanuel. That meeting now seemed an eternity ago, whereas it had been only a few weeks. So much had happened.

On the positive side, he'd manoeuvred himself into a key position going forward. After the problems had settled down and they had moved to the new building, he would ask Aaron for a pay rise.

Smiling to himself, he imagined clearing his debts. Jumping on a bus, he picked up a discarded copy of the Sun and checked the sports news, but his mind drifted. The attempt to impede the smooth running of the servers had been clever. Her programming skills, with no one aware of the direction she had taken, bordered on phenomenal. She had set her voice to live before the accident. With no incident, what had she planned for the Monday morning when they met? His mind whirled. No thinking outside of the box could reveal her plan for the small business that she had joined.

His only hope of an explanation would not come from Evelyn, although he had not plucked up the courage to visit her. A woman he fancied lay clinging to life in a coma. Should he or shouldn't he visit? The issue nagged at him. His uncle, who he had never liked, had lectured him frequently about duty. To be true to himself, he had considered it as ramblings from an old soldier, but it was his duty to do the best for the woman he had wished to seduce. He shuddered.

Trying to distract his mind, he hoped that Sadie had found information in Scarborough that could put the background of Evelyn into context. Although he had worked late, he'd have time for a pint and steak in a Sheffield town centre pub before catching the tram to his rooms in Malin Bridge. His mobile rang. Glancing at the screen, he smiled and pushed the answer button.

'Hi, Sadie.'

'Help me, Dan. I can't cope.' Gulping and sobbing emanated from his phone.

'What's happened? Where are you?'

Another gulp, 'In my flat, I've arrived home.'

The bus from the office to the town centre was near to Chapeltown. 'I'm on my way. Next stop, mate.'

The driver shook his head and swerved into the bus stop. Dan shuffled, waiting for the door to open.

Setting off at a sprint, he panted heavily but didn't stop. He'd been to the gym since he settled into his job with Aaron, so he maintained a steady pace despite his weight. With aching legs, he turned the corner of the street where she lived. The front room had lights. Gasping for breath, he banged on the door of the end of the terrace house. It opened immediately. Sadie sobbed and shivered, although wearing an outside jacket. 'Oh, Dan.' She put her hand out to steady herself against the wall of the small entrance hall. Tears streamed down her cheeks from her puffy eyes and she swallowed air rapidly.

Stepping into the passage, he closed the door behind

him. 'What's happened, Sadie?'

'It's Evelyn, I can't cope.' Sadie's face paled. His arm caught her as she slid down the wall.

Reaching for her waist, he carried her into the lounge and set her in the armchair. 'Tell me what's happened. Settle yourself first and take your time.'

'I bought a new phone and entered the numbers manually as I couldn't stand the thought of Evelyn's voice speaking directly to me as she had done in the office.'

'What happened?'

'I arrived home and intended to ring you to explain what happened in Scarborough when her picture appeared on the screen.'

'Did it speak?'

'No,' sniffed Sadie.

'Calm yourself, I'll investigate. Give me your phone.' She settled, although remaining pale and twitchy.

Flicking through the settings on her phone, he spent a few minutes pressing buttons. He'd knelt in front of Sadie.

'Can you see what caused it?' She gulped.

Dan nodded. 'One phone within the business had not been cleaned of Evelyn's apps. It's sending a corrupt app with the picture to everyone else in the address book which is then forwarded.'

He flicked his own phone on. He didn't show Sadie, but a picture of Evelyn came onto his screen. He took hold of Sadie's hand.

Tears streamed down her face. 'When will the haunting stop?'

'There are no other words. Evelyn is evil. But I'm determined to work out how she has hacked the computers and phones. We might never discover what she intended, but I'm convinced we can put an end to it. I need to find the phone that caused the problem, then clean it down. I guess it belongs to either Candice or Ahmed.'

'Simon became distraught about the image of Evelyn he received.'

He patted her hand. 'Yes, he told me this morning, so we worked on the systems and found the hidden images and I've dealt with them. Everyone else will receive this one but I can remove them.'

'That would be a relief, Dan.'

'Do you want me to check the other equipment you have?'

'Not now. I'm too tired, but I won't sleep. No chance.'

Dan glanced at his watch. 'It's only eight o'clock. You need a stiff drink and there's a good pub at the bottom of the road.'

Sadie gave him a weak smile as they left her flat. He waited for her to take deep breaths of fresh air. 'Thanks, Dan, I have faith in what you say, as your technical skills are unbelievable. But for how long will she dominate our lives?'

He caught her hand. 'She will be gone from our lives within days. I've lost all sympathy for her and will destroy her technical legacy. She is a maniac and I will rid our lives of her. You, me and Simon form a good team.'

She gave the briefest of smiles. 'Yes, we do.'

'Within a short time, Aaron and Ahmed need to prove their worth to us otherwise my idea would be for the three of us to form our own business.'

She linked her arm into his. 'That would be wonderful.'

Arriving at the pub door, the warm atmosphere spilling out greeted them. They served steak. Perfect, as he was hungry. 'The most difficult person is Candice.'

Sadie gave the first genuine smile of the evening, 'Why?'

She seems to pull the strings in the background. She is not as daft and flitty as she appears.

42

Candice settled into her new bright red Ziani Model F, 'Destination, TechMatt at Chapeltown.' The car gradually moved out of the drive and pulled away. The gates closed automatically behind it. She set the top speed of twenty-five miles per hour to suit the morning rush hour traffic. She wanted Sadie's new program to tailor the speed and acceleration to personal comfort factors. Lazily holding the steering wheel, she flicked the voice control button, 'Dial Ahmed.'

Ignoring the traffic, she let the car make the judgements as it glided to a halt at an amber light and stopped as it turned red. 'Hello.'

Ahmed wouldn't have her new number, so she didn't receive his gruff greeting.

'Hello, Ahmed, it's time we had a chat.'

'What about?'

She had grown accustomed to the aggressive tone but ignored it. 'I want to make sure the funding stays with TechMatt. I know you from the past, you'll pull out when you've lost interest.'

'I wanted to be close to you, so that's the only reason I invested. In the hospital after our car crash, you made it clear our relationship is over.'

'It is, but I told you I wanted the finance to continue.'

'You don't understand how money works, Candice. I'm returning to work after three weeks absence because of the crash. The funding for Aaron is not a top priority, but when I reach it on my to-do list, then I'm withdrawing. Aaron and you will have to find someone else to milk, as I'm never coming back to TechMatt. I shall cut my ties with Aaron.'

'Where are you now?'

'On my yacht at Monte Carlo, I'm working remotely.'

'The attraction of that lifestyle no longer appealed. Too precarious, but holidays there would be brill. In a year Ahmed would mellow and invite her but wouldn't get her into bed. Those days were over. She smiled.

Her car quietly slid into a parking bay at the new headquarters of TechMatt.

'Did the police talk to you about the trip you had with Evelyn?'

A long silence followed. She waited. 'It's long gone, they must have concluded an accident.' The tone of his bravado hadn't fooled her.

Candice leaned forward in her seat and raised her head to the microphone above. 'Listen to me, Ahmed. And listen carefully.'

'What?'

'The police told me yesterday it is still an open case.'

'Why did they want to speak to you?'

'Ongoing enquiries. They asked if I could remember anything else leading up to Evelyn's injury.'

'What did you say?' She noted the edge of tension with a self-satisfied smirk.

She had Ahmed's total attention. 'That if I remembered anything, I would contact them.' A smug expression worked its way across her face as she sensed unnerving him. Another long silence at the other end. Ahmed would be linking back to their previous conversation.

'You wouldn't stoop that low.'

'The business needs to succeed.' Her voice was low pitched and cold. 'If TechMatt grows and makes money I continue my lifestyle and stay with Aaron, also you will receive the return on your money.'

'And if I withdraw?'

'The business will fail. I will lose my house and probably my husband and it will be your fault. So, you know what I will do?'

Ahmed hissed, 'That's blackmail.'

She smiled into the phone, 'Ahmed, why don't you give Aaron a ring and confirm the future money plans are in place.'

The line went dead.

The business could not be left to Aaron to run as he had made too many wrong decisions. The problem she faced was her lack of knowledge of technical matters, but there were plenty around who understood. She would consider her options. Aaron had erred in choosing Ahmed. Did he realise the man might be rich but couldn't be trusted? How had the obvious slipped past him?

Candice stepped from her car as Sadie pedalled into the car park. Sadie's face was alive with expectation, 'The first of the new staff arrive today, but I've never managed a team before.'

'I'm sure your enthusiasm and knowledge will overcome your lack of experience.'

'I hope so. Everything has changed dramatically in the last three weeks. The Evelyn viruses terrified me, but Dan cleared them.'

'My phone was the last trigger although I didn't realise.' Candice adjusted the cuffs of her new jacket. Sadie tucked her bike in the rack and padlocked it before opening the front door of the building. 'A rumour tells me you and Dan are together.'

Sadie giggled. 'Yes, since the night he came to my flat after the image of Evelyn appeared.'

'That's great news. He's a good man.' The wide space of the new office floor in Chapeltown had shoulder high dividers formed of elaborate planters and screens. Sadie approached a group of four desks with her name displayed on the entrance to the area.

Candice strolled around the outside of the pods and stopped at Simon's name. He sat alone with full concentration on his typing and the array of data displayed on the screen, so she pulled up a chair.

'Hello, Simon.' He finished typing the sentence before turning his head, but his hands hovered over the keyboard. 'I can understand you were fed up with me a time ago, but we need to resume a normal working relationship.'

'Do we?'

'Yes, I'm chatting with Aaron about becoming involved in the business and even working part-time here.'

'Why are you telling me? That's nothing to do with me.'

'The past is over. Can we work together?'

'I'm sure there won't be any necessity for you and me to be on the same team.' Simon resumed his typing.

She frowned at his dismissive attitude. 'It's your problem, not mine.' Pushing back the chair, she strolled to her husband's office who sat behind his desk studying his screen.

'Hello, darling.' His face creased into a broad welcoming smile. 'Great news. Ahmed has rung to confirm the money going forward.'

'That's excellent. So, he must be back at work.'

'Yes. It was a quick call and he seemed in a strange mood, but he confirmed the money.'

She glanced away towards the window, as she couldn't suppress the complacent smile that tweaked at her lips. Once composed, she dropped onto a chair in front of his desk. 'I've nothing in my diary for the next week, so I'm available to help. The new recruits will arrive today, won't they?'

'Your availability is a surprise but a pleasant one. You can be a great help, darling.'

The smile dropped away from her face. 'Have you heard any news about Evelyn?'

'I'd much prefer nothing more to do with her after the anguish she has caused. But as the police are still involved, I have arranged with the Sergeant and hospital that I will seek an update on Monday mornings.'

'That's sensible. What did they say this morning?'

'She is sleeping a great deal and progress is slow, but she is becoming more aware of her surroundings. That's little change since last week. They emphasised she may never recover.'

43

Aaron relaxed in his chair at the head of the table in his office. 'Thank you for coming to this meeting on a Saturday. Especially to Ahmed, who has flown back to join us today. We have been busy in the month since we moved into the Chapeltown building. Without doubt, the new triangle of products is superb.'

Ahmed narrowed his eyes as a look of uncertainty flashed across his features. 'Will we be having a demonstration to convince me?'

'Yes, Ahmed. Each of the team leaders, Simon, Sadie and Dan, will demonstrate their contributions. As I have helped with the integration, I will show this meeting how they work together.'

'When will the products be ready for the market rather than on desk computers?'

Aaron grinned. 'I have the perfect answer for you, Ahmed?'

'You do?'

'When we have finished in the office later this morning, we will use Candice's and my new Ziani to travel home for lunch. You will see the integration between the cars and the home environment. Thanks to Candice's hard work in user testing, you will be amazed at what has been achieved.' She smiled across at her husband and her face flushed.

'We started funding when you first heard Dess. I will ask Sadie to take us through the new version, which is improved from the original. The computer screen at the end of the room came to life as Dan passed the remote keyboard and mouse to Sadie.

'Thanks, Aaron. Simon will help me with the technical details if I become stuck.'

The logo of TechMatt appeared on the screen. Sadie typed, Dess.

'Sorry, guys. Listen to me, this cannot happen.' The shrill disembodied voice of Evelyn bounced around the room.

Sadie screamed.

Ahmed's eyes opened wide. 'Evelyn! She is a ghost.'

Dan leaped to his feet, crashing into the table and pushing back his chair. 'Where the bloody hell has she come from? I'll check the server room.'

Aaron put his head in his hands. 'My God! What is happening? I thought she'd gone.'

Ahmed stood up. 'I'm leaving.'

Candice sprung to her feet, 'You are not until we understand what has happened, she's been gone for weeks. It's only your appearance this morning that has re-introduced her. Perhaps it's one of your underhand tricks because we're successful.'

Ahmed's wide eyes blinked repeatedly. 'What are you on about?'

Simon shouted over the din, 'Sit down. Be sensible, it's a glitch. Dan will discover the cause as we cleaned the systems completely.'

Ahmed shouted, 'I'm not standing for this! You can't issue orders to me.'

Dan reappeared in the doorway with a smile on his face and blocked Ahmed's route.

Aaron hoped Dan had an answer. 'What has happened?'

'It's Ahmed.'

'Don't be so ridiculous! Why would I want to resurrect Evelyn?'

Everyone in the office had stood.

'Explain please, Dan.' He hoped it wouldn't be back to square one with Evelyn.

Dan rubbed his beard. 'The monitoring system is good and it's vastly different to when we started. The computer that came onto the network this morning introduced the Evelyn virus again. That means it must be Ahmed's laptop, as it's the only addition. He's used it in the past in this office and must have picked up the virus when it first started, it's timed like a trojan horse, so he reintroduced it to the system.'

'Why didn't the system find the virus when he attached

to the network.'

'He'd only connected as the meeting started. The scan hadn't covered all his discs, so it escaped and played, but has already been cleaned from the system.'

'How can we be sure it won't occur again?'

'I registered all the computers that had accessed our system and tracked them all but one. Ahmed normally uses his iPad, not his laptop.'

Aaron waved his hand in a calming motion. 'Relax everyone, it's over.' He glanced at the wall clock. 'As of eleven o'clock this morning Evelyn has been destroyed.'

'I hope so,' Candice breathed deeply and fiddled with her phone.

Aaron smiled, 'Come on everyone, it's over. Never again. Let's check our machines, which will give everyone confidence and then we can settle to the meeting.'

Candice moved to the door. 'I can't concentrate yet. Give it half an hour, Aaron, it will allow everyone to calm and then we will focus.'

Sadie flicked her hand, 'Yes, please, Aaron, it came as a shock.'

Aaron nodded at Ahmed, 'Will you allow everyone time to calm?'

He nodded and muttered, 'I'll fetch a coffee, then I'll see what has happened to my laptop.'

44

Dan frowned as he reviewed the server screen. The incident had been a test of his expertise in securing the system. His life had risen to a high after his relationship with Sadie had developed. He'd always wanted a long-term relationship and he hoped she felt the same. His security system for TechMatt had developed from in-depth research, which he had never undertaken at Uni. If the business failed, he had a range of demonstrable skills to offer.

The lights buzzing showed the checking of all computers. Pulling the keyboard in front of him, he studied the dashboard for the servers and the connected equipment. The log showed the attempted invasion from Ahmed's machine, but it had been stopped and eradicated. It would be the last of Evelyn's legacy.

A smile spread across his face, as he'd managed the situation well. The last month had proved his worth to the business.

A gentle tap came on the door. 'Are you in there, Dan?'

'Yep.'

Sadie opened the door enough to squeeze through. Putting her arm around him, she kissed him on the cheek. 'How is the system working? Evelyn is not back to haunt us, is she?'

Placing his arm around Sadie's waist, he drew her towards him. 'The dashboard is green, she's gone and will never return.'

Sadie kissed him lightly on the lips. 'I'll leave you to your computers and join the others.' She squeezed his arm and slipped out of the cupboard. As she left, a smile creased his face.

Dan closed the dashboard screen and brought up his own account. The orange email icon showed '1' next to it. He didn't receive many emails on a Saturday so it would be advertising or from Aaron, so he flicked open his inbox.

The sender of the email was Evelyn Chumley at TechMatt.com. He froze as his mind raced. A shiver ran through him. Where had it come from? Flicking at the keyboard, the source revealed to be from outside his business. He spotted the wrong web address. TechMatt didn't have a dash in the middle.

His finger hovered over the open button, but he switched back to the dashboard and to the incoming router. It took him a couple of minutes to trace the source of the email. It had come from an internet hosting company in the US. Had Evelyn set up a lookalike account in the States?

His stomach churned and he broke out in a sweat despite the chill of the server room. Wiping his hand down the side of his jeans, he traced the hosting company. His heart sank as it appeared perfectly reputable. His mind raced. It would make it hard to shut down her phantom site if the hosting was by a legitimate company. Could his be an isolated email? He took a deep breath because he guessed not. Would Evelyn's presence start again?

In a few keystrokes, he returned to his email account. He checked the screen. No attachments that could cause problems, so he clicked Open to discover a long wordy message.

Dan

You were paying attention to me.

Some of your attentions were not complimentary.

The persistent emails about attractiveness and how you wanted to meet me out of work were unwanted.

Even worse were the monitors you put in my house.

I set them up so I could tell when you were watching them.

It's not pleasant to know you were snooping on me late in the evening.

Your actions towards me would be called stalking.

Dan shifted his eyes away from the screen. His hands shook. Fear skittered up his spine and beads of cold sweat formed on his forehead. Who else had this been sent to? It appeared to be only addressed to him. Evelyn lay in a hospital bed and incapable, so it must be a timed email. How much more? He forced himself to read the rest of the email.

Then Dan you dropped the invites and tried to ingratiate

yourself.

You became worried that Aaron wanted to sack you, so hoped to attach yourself to me.

That's deceitful.

So far, a deceitful stalker, that's not very pleasant, is it?

Questions for you to think about Dan.

'Was Candice good fun or was she too drunk after the charity dinner?'

And the second question. 'What would Aaron do if he found out you'd been with his wife?'

You never showed me any respect. Why should I be loyal to you?

Panic jabbed at him. Why had she sent this? Would it be an idle threat? This was blackmail. What would she want for her silence? Guilt gripped him. Her words were true. His body became rigid. There was one more line to read, and he had to force himself.

This is a timed email. If you have received it, then something has happened to me. Either I'm seriously injured or dead. Were you responsible?

Dan put his face in his hands. He would be sacked. If Evelyn had sent this to Aaron, he would contact the police. Dan would have to prove his location on the afternoon Evelyn had been injured. That would be difficult, as he didn't want to admit what he'd been doing. He let out a harsh breath. Would he become a suspect?

45

Simon screwed his eyes shut and his hands covered his ears. The evil voice had again penetrated his brain. Could he not escape the witch? Why haunt him? The others were frightened of the voice, but he had become terrified.

Was there no escape from her enveloping spells? He must make sure she is finally dead in his mind. Shaking his head, he attempted to dispel the eternal evil. Flicking on his computer, he would check on Dan's progress. Entire green on the security dashboard. Dan had done well, but would he have stifled the malevolent spirit forever?

Evelyn loved cat and mouse games. Since she joined the business, it had become a huge sport for her, but she wanted to take over and change the rules to force them all into submission. But did she have an ultimate aim? What malicious intent was on her mind? Wishing she was dead, he could not muster an ounce of empathy for her as she lay in her hospital bed. Perhaps her villainous behaviour from before joining TechMatt had caught up with her.

Simon groaned. He had to shake himself from his vengeful mood. Aaron had told him his team leader role would be promoted to Technical Director when the next round of funding became available, which would happen today with Ahmed's presence at the meeting.

Pride at his achievements caused a satisfied smile to etch its way across his lips. He checked the office. Sadie had come from the computer room and had returned to Aaron's office. Candice and Ahmed hadn't moved from there. Aaron stood in the kitchen pouring a cup of coffee. Dan remained in the computer room.

Simon, bored with waiting, clicked on his emails. One of them stood out on the list that had arrived in his inbox, but he spotted the wrong website name, which had the hyphen. He swallowed deeply. Evelyn's name pulsed before his eyes.

How could there be an email from Evelyn? He quickly thought it through. From an external site. He rubbed the back of his neck as the Fitbit on his wrist vibrated. His heart thumped. He couldn't ignore the email. Would this be the final part of her behaviour to undermine him? With a trembling finger, he flicked it open while tension gnawed at his gut. What would he find?

Simon

I know you read my emails.

You would have guessed from the emails about Aaron and me that we were having an affair.

It was nasty and underhand to go through my emails and Sadie's.

You are so insecure you needed to check the emails of everyone in the business.

It didn't come as a surprise you were so tired the following day.

I wanted you to own up and make some excuse.

But you didn't.

Simon rubbed his face. She had shifted her attack on him. His job was on the line. There would be no promotion if Aaron found out. Had Evelyn stored the evidence. No, she couldn't have. This must be a bluff. He read on to confirm his supposition.

You liked Sadie's suggestion that I'd raised the alarm because I'd been caught out reading her emails.

I created a problem for you, didn't I, Simon?

You wanted me out, so your top job would be secure, but you wanted me as your woman.

The anguish of trying to reconcile the two made you anxious and stressed.

I knew but had no sympathy.

You are a precise man who only goes with certainty.

But I can't forgive you for following me that night.

You remember, don't you?

You followed me down the motorway to Doncaster.

You wanted to make sure about me meeting Aaron.

Were you going to blackmail Aaron or me?

I guessed how your mind would work.

First, you would blackmail me so you could have sex, and then you would blackmail Aaron, forcing him to promote you to the top job.

What about those evenings you followed me home and sat outside in your car?

I could see it in your eyes that night we met and shared the Bud.

You would have sex with me whether or not I wanted to.

That's true, isn't it, Simon?

So, you are an obsessive secretive stalker who had sex on his mind.

I think you'll agree, that is not a pleasant description.

This is a timed email.

If you have received it, then something has happened to me.

Either I'm seriously injured or dead. Were you responsible?

He closed his eyes to stifle the emotion and to think logically. Would it only be him? No. She would have targeted Dan as well as he hassled her. What about Sadie accusing her of stealing the bracelet? Other people would receive emails. Evelyn wouldn't restrict it to him. How had she discovered he'd been following her? He thought he'd been discreet. His shoulders slumped and he cast his eyes downwards as his mind became overwhelmed by his stupidity. She had been tracking him and his car. It could not be only him. Just in case there are no others, he pressed delete. The end of Evelyn.

46

Sadie smiled as she left the computer room, happy beyond her dreams. Dan had become a brill boyfriend, so caring and attentive. She wouldn't have believed her life could have been transformed into a super job and a relationship, both of which held so much promise.

Drifting towards Aaron's office, she was keen for the meeting to start, but her stomach churned. The tension of hearing Evelyn's voice again had unsettled her, but she trusted Dan to resolve the problem. He took matters calmly and logically, which is more than she could do, but his attitude gave her a sense of perspective. Simon sat at his desk with a hunched posture. He stared intensely at his computer through narrowed eyes, but he often did that, and he didn't raise his head.

Any spark of his interest towards her had disappeared when she started dating Dan. Aaron stood in the small kitchen area talking on his phone. Sadie returned to take her seat in Aaron's office. Neither Ahmed nor Candice looked up from their computers as she settled herself. The waiting made her bored.

Facebook beckoned. No, she'd be positive and clear her emails.

The colour drained from her face. Her hands shook. What would it say? Why had she sent it? A shiver ran like a ghostly touch over her skin and a sense of dread rolled through her as she clicked it open.

Sadie

Let me first say how sorry I am about your bracelet.

Sadie closed the email. Despite what she thought about her, the poor woman lay in a hospital bed. Even if she lived, would she ever recover? The message was a voice from the grave. She'd only read the first part, but the sentence echoed in her mind. Evelyn had taken the bracelet. Sadie had no pleasure in finding out her supposition had been correct. Could she read the rest of it? She tried to compose herself and settle her stomach and nerves, but her hand shook as she clicked the email open again.

You found out I had a problem.

I'd been hiding it for a long time.

One time, I overheard Simon and Dan talking about you and the bracelet.

They supported me because of the good clothes I wore.

You've probably guessed, but I got them the same way as the bracelet.

If you're receiving this email, it doesn't matter if you tell anyone you were right.

I'm sure I'm not in a position to worry about it.

Sadie gulped and fought back the nausea. The sweat poured down her back. Her hands shook uncontrollably. She glanced at Candice and Ahmed, but neither had taken any notice of her. They stared at their screen with an intensity she'd never seen before in either of them. Had they received an email? If so, what was the message? She shook her head, pushing the thoughts aside. They were unimportant. She had to reach the end of the one she'd received.

You'd installed your own monitor, which gave me the idea.

I found it hard deflecting your accusations, but since I gave up alcohol, I could think clearer.

That's why I never wanted to spend an evening with you.

But I couldn't leave you alone.

I must apologise again to you.

Once you made the first accusation, I had to know what you planned.

I put a monitor on your machine which would send me everything you did on your computer.

I knew you'd found out about me and changed your approach, which struck me as kind.

Unfortunately, I didn't catch on for a while what you were doing.

Your emotional analysis I found annoying, but you were listening to everyone as well.

That was underhand, Sadie.

You couldn't be trusted not to snoop.

Will Aaron keep you on when he finds out that you've been listening to everything he has said?

This is a timed email. If you have received it, then something has happened to me. Either I'm seriously injured or dead. Were you responsible?

Sadie lurched from her desk with her hand clutched across her mouth, ignoring the looks of Candice and Ahmed, she scampered across the outer office to the Ladies Toilet.

47

Candice sent a text saying she couldn't make a hen weekend in Spain. She had been amazed at how she'd settled to work in the business. The days of jumping into a man's bed at the slightest opportunity or passing fancy had gone. She glanced across at Ahmed. It wouldn't be long before the business would be self-sustaining and then he and his money could disappear into oblivion. Her manipulation of Ahmed had been straightforward.

A smirk of malicious amusement hovered on her lips. The man was a wimp; he had no backbone and had caved in so easily to minimal pressure. Why was he so nervous about police involvement? What was he hiding? Did he have a secret? As he was no longer of use to her, she dismissed him from her mind. The decision to stick with Aaron had been the right course of action, despite his wanderings in the past.

She had emails from new staff and her eyes travelled down the list. Which one first? One stood out. Her stomach knotted and her shoulders tensed. So, she's back again.

Will none of these men relieve me of the torment of the evil woman? Evelyn's affair with Aaron had shaken her. At one point, she thought she might lose him to the siren and that her marriage would collapse. Her thoughts brought up the hairs on the back of her neck. She would have fought tooth and nail to save her marriage and would not have relaxed back and allowed Evelyn to snare him away. She opened the email. Candice would never have sympathy for Evelyn.

Hi Candice,

I've not much to say to you.

We were never destined to be friends and we were not.

But an apology is in order.

I'm sorry I had sex with your husband, but with Ahmed and Dan in your sights and hoping for Simon, I didn't suppose you would mind.

How was the charity dinner?

You and Dan!

That surprised me.

This is a timed email. If you have received it, then something has happened to me. Either I'm seriously injured or dead.

Were you responsible?

A cold shaft of terror assailed her, so powerful that she sank back into the chair. For several long seconds she remained frozen, unable to think or move. Then, in one swift movement, she deleted the email. Should she confess her indiscretions to Aaron? Perhaps it would be best. Dan had matched with Sadie, so one complication had gone away, but the few times with him had been good. A warm blush spread across her cheeks. His love making had been both passionate and sensitive.

The affair with Simon had never started. The thrill of the chase had satisfied her needs.

Ahmed was out of the picture. Over the years, the illicit meetings with him had thrilled her and she'd always wanted more. But he no longer ignited any passion in her and his usefulness to her was finished.

Yes, she would give a quiet confession to Aaron over dinner when they were both relaxed with a glass of wine. He can admit Evelyn and then they could go forward. However, she would not mention Ahmed. Aaron would kick her out if he knew it had happened many times over the years.

If Evelyn has dug up the dirt on me, what about the others? We will need to put a few skeletons in the cupboard before we can move on. Now when will this damned meeting start?

48

Aaron finished a call while standing in the kitchen. It had been a shock with Evelyn earlier, but Dan had warned him it might happen. That line of hassle was dead and buried. It was time to make progress. He'd given the others time to check their machines and settle down from the upset.

He passed the back of Simon, who strangely stared as though in a trance at a blank screen. 'Simon, let's start again. Can you get Dan?'

Simon stood but didn't speak. Sadie crossed the floor of the office. 'Are you okay, Sadie? You are pale.'

'Breakfast disagreed with me.' He followed her into his office. Candice and Ahmed didn't look up. He flicked at his computer and spotted the email which stood out from the others. His lips straightened and his shoulders tensed. A false website address, but he had little doubt the email had been timed and would be from Evelyn. This could become tricky. He opened it.

Aaron

You didn't think that I liked you, did you?

I've had a bad past but needed a job.

Sorry about the forged documents, but I guess you wanted me, so didn't look too hard at them.

I became hopeful.

The others, Simon and Dan, I could deal with.

But then I could see it in your eyes.

They were as clear as any I'd ever seen before. Sleep with me or you're sacked.

I didn't mind at first, but then your attention transferred to Sadie and you thought about sacking me.

I couldn't have that.

Why should your business be successful if I wasn't there?

I'd always wanted an insurance, so I integrated in my own way.

From the beginning you spotted something in me, which is why you didn't give me the team leader role.

Sorry Aaron, but I couldn't let you succeed without me.

Ahmed, Candice, and even you wanted me out.

This is a timed email. If you have received it, then something has happened to me.

Either I'm seriously injured or dead.

Were you responsible?

Aaron glanced up from the screen. The others would have received messages. Sadie sat slumped in her chair. Her wide, frightened eyes convinced him. A solemn expression had replaced her early morning bouncy and giggly self. Simon stood in the doorway, still and sullen, rather than the positive outlook he'd had recently. Evelyn had sent a message to all.

The frown on Candice's face told him what he wanted. She nodded. They understood each other. He followed Candice's eyes to Ahmed who smiled at the screen of his laptop. Neither could see what he enjoyed. 'Ahmed, check your emails.'

49

Ahmed frowned at Aaron. He didn't enjoy receiving orders. After all, he was the one who controlled the money and determined whether the business would be successful. He shouldn't have come today. He focused on Candice. What a mistake to revive the old days with her. It had been easy sex in the past, so why had she changed? There was no way she'd become loyal to Aaron. Candice and her scheming must be removed from his life. Which email? He clicked.

Ahmed

You thought me an easy time girl that would fall for your charm.

The same as your women in the past.

I don't know who they were, but if the police ask Candice, I'm sure she will know.

I stopped in the woods that night when you asked.

Despite you forcing your hand up my skirt, I resolved to resist you.

But you don't like a woman saying no to you.

It wasn't kind to threaten me with the sack, unless I did what you wanted.

You expected to win, but you didn't.

I concocted that surprise to come up on the screen of your Ziani.

Tricky to implement but the result pleased me.

I used Dan's app to make sure the message would only appear on your screen over 70mph.

I expect it gave you a fright!

I know how your mind works.

Your word against mine?

By the way, I recorded our evening together.

This is a timed email. If you have received it, then something has happened to me.

Either I'm seriously injured or dead.

Were you responsible?

Ahmed opened his eyes wide. What had Aaron and Candice done to him? They were blackmailers. Candice had led him on, but never delivered what he wanted. She'd told him she would stay loyal to Aaron. He should have guessed that they had collaborated to siphon his money away. He understood their planned deception of him.

He pushed back his chair, which collided heavily with the wall as he jumped to his feet. Simon and Dan stood in the doorway with grim faces. Were they all in it together? They wanted his money. He must escape. 'I'm not staying here a moment longer. I'll never speak to any of you again.'

Grabbing his laptop, he slammed it shut and took his first step to the door. Aaron jumped as Dan shouted, 'Sit down, Ahmed. We've all received a private message from Evelyn. I'm sure they are all unpleasant.'

The authoritative and harsh tone had come from the broad-shouldered man blocking his way. He was too large to tackle. Perhaps he was the dishonest one. He studied the other faces.

Their eyes focused on him. I'm being stitched up and the enormous guy is threatening me.

Candice snapped, 'Ahmed, sit down. We need to stop Evelyn. Running away from that bitch will not be the solution. I don't need the technical guys to tell me this set of emails is from outside and will be much harder to stop.'

50

Simon slumped into a chair. 'Candice is right. We must collaborate. She must be stopped.'

His Fitbit wouldn't stop buzzing, so he stripped it from his wrist and threw it on the table. His mind raced. Could he admit receiving a bad email without revealing the contents? If the accusations became common knowledge, he would be sacked and reported to the police. He must prevent Evelyn's allegations from becoming known but had to admit to unpleasantness. It wouldn't be easy.

Sadie whimpered, 'She's haunting us. I can't stand it any longer.' She glanced at Dan standing in the doorway. Her only hope of privacy would be through him. 'Why have you done this to us, Evelyn?'

Dan stood in the doorway, pointing at Ahmed. 'You are going nowhere. We are all in it together. Sit! Don't point that finger at me unless you fancy taking me on.' Dan slumped into his seat near the door.

Ahmed, stunned by the vehemence of the outburst, slunk back to his seat and slumped down. 'The bitch is evil. She must be stopped.'

A harrowing headache pounded at Simon's forehead and a nervous tic had begun at the corner of his eye. Would this nightmare ever end?

Aaron's tense voice cut through his misery and reverberated through the room. 'I thought we'd killed her off.'

51

A clear and resonant female voice filled the room. 'You are correct. Evelyn has been killed.'

Sergeant Mulgrave stepped from the doorway into the room, 'This morning at eleven o'clock, Evelyn died from her injuries.' She strode into the room, which had become silent. Pacing around the group, who sat at the elongated table, her face contorted to a snarl. She let the uneasy quiet continue. No one would speak. All eyes watched her with startled intensity. The floor was hers.

Stopping behind Aaron's chair, the intense expression never left her face. 'Many of you will not be aware that the authorities and especially the police do not like cases that are labelled unexplained. The crux of our investigation focused on whether Evelyn succumbed to a sad and terrible accident or a deliberate act of violence.'

Conscious that all eyes in the room would follow her movement, she wanted to prolong this part of the investigation, hoping someone would give her an indisputable clue. A confession would be too much to hope for. She shifted her position and, in a slow and deliberate manner, she studied the faces of the six people sat at the table. Without exception, they looked worried and uncomfortable. What were they hiding? Did one of them hold the key to this investigation, or were they all involved?

'Several pathologists have been consulted, and they have advised the police that the injury could not have been sustained in an accident, therefore I'm sure you can reach the same conclusion as me.'

The gasps in the room crackled. No one spoke. The silence hung in the air, eerily strange and unnerving. With slow precision, she completed a second circuit of the motionless group. Stopping, 'Given that Evelyn led a lonely life with no known activities away from this business, I can inform you ladies and gentlemen that you are at the heart of a murder enquiry.'

52

Sadie whimpered. 'My God, poor Evelyn. God rest her soul.' She clutched Dan's hand as tears flowed down her cheeks. She struggled to balance the sympathy she had given Evelyn when her background became known to the haunting and vindictive email she had received.

Ahmed's arrogant and high-pitched voice rang out across the room, 'It's nothing to do with me, I want a lawyer.'

Candice shouted, 'Shut up, Ahmed. The police are being overdramatic. They arrived with unfortunate timing. Evelyn worked for us. Nothing more. No one here was involved with the attack on her.'

Sadie doubted those around her. She would have been willing to help Evelyn with her problems, but the dead woman had resisted social interaction. The men would have found her attractive. Perhaps her vindictiveness caused one of them to take the ultimate step and attack her.

She shuddered as Dan's obsession with Evelyn sprang back to her mind, but a glance at her boyfriend showed no anxiety on his face. She knew him well, as they had been lovers for many weeks. He hadn't attacked Evelyn, but could she be sure? Evelyn's evil had forced someone in this room to take the ultimate step.

Her eyes settled on Candice. Perhaps her assumption that it would be a man was wrong. Had Candice discovered Aaron's affair with Evelyn and killed her as she returned the car on that fateful afternoon?

Her eyes lingered on those at the table. Ahmed had a nasty temper. Had Evelyn tried to blackmail him for his money. With her new knowledge of Evelyn, it would be a possibility.

Sadie shook her head as she must give up speculating. Her only hope would be that the police could solve the death of Evelyn quickly. But her mind wouldn't stop racing at the suspects. Simon? She couldn't be sure and then her eyes fixed on Aaron. Perhaps Evelyn wanted to be more than a mistress. She was lying and deceitful, so why not take Aaron for a ride.

Perhaps he had found out and killed her.

Her eyes settled on him. Aaron had become her lover. For a short time, she had been infatuated with him. She shuddered as she focused, but he wouldn't make eye contact.

Her eyes circled around the pale faces. Which one of them is guilty? What drove that person to take such an extreme step? Murder. The word circled around in her head and a strange, muzzy sensation engulfed her.

53

Aaron gulped. How much had the police heard? His comment had been badly timed. It could be misinterpreted. He plastered a false smile on his face and waved his arm in a welcoming gesture. Other police officers waited in the outer office. 'Thank you for telling us the tragic news. As you can see, we are in the middle of a business meeting.'

The Sergeant came to the edge of the table. She scrutinised each one. Another man in jeans and a sweat top entered and took a position behind her. Two police constables matching Dan's build stepped into the office and stood to either side of the door. Aaron eyed the newcomers and shuffled in his chair.

'Mr Matthews, you may assume your business meeting is at an end.' The Sergeant's hollow voice echoed in the room. A flash of irritation and impatience shone in her eyes.

Ahmed wiped a hand across his forehead and pushed back his chair. 'I have done nothing wrong. I do not need to stay so I shall bid you good morning and be on my way.'

The two uniform constables stepped across the doorway and glowered in his direction. He sank slowly back down onto his seat with a loud, exasperated sigh. Why was Ahmed jittery? What secrets did he have?

A silence ensued that the Sergeant did not break. She raised her hands, palms down, showing all should return to their seats. 'You have been asked about your whereabouts on the Sunday afternoon when the murder took place.'

Aaron shivered at the word murder. 'It is my current belief that everyone in this room lied to the police or left out crucial information that would have assisted us. Protecting a criminal who is found guilty of murder is a serious offence and the court will always give a custodial sentence. Unless I get immediate cooperation, I shall charge everyone with conspiracy to pervert the course of justice.'

Aaron drew in a stuttered gasp at her threatening words and tried to swallow the sudden bile that had risen in his throat. No one moved. No one spoke. The hum of the computer filled the atmosphere.

54

Dan placed the palms of his hands down on the table in front of him and cleared his throat. 'Sergeant. This cannot continue. I've never been an angel in my life.' Sadie clutched his hand. 'But being tied up in a murder investigation where I am a suspect is something I cannot cope with. I can tell you everyone in this room received a timed email from Evelyn this morning. If they are like mine, they hit hard at the truth. How Evelyn discovered the information is difficult to find out, but she has been highly intelligent and very resourceful.'

'Thank you, Mr Harding.'

Sadie gulped. 'I received an email this morning. The implications are terrifying.'

'Thank you, Ms Joiner.'

Ahmed banged his fist on the table and leapt to his feet. 'I did not. I'm not part of this business and do not know of the ins and outs of what has been happening here. You have no right to keep me here.'

The Sergeant sneered, 'I'm arresting you for attempting to pervert the course of justice. You do not have to say anything. But it may harm your defence if you do not mention when questioned something which you later rely on in court. Anything you say may be given in evidence.' She paused. A wince of terror flickered across Ahmed's face and he wilted. 'Sit down and listen to me.' Dan stared across at Ahmed whose brown eyes were dilated with fear. What was he hiding? Why was he so frightened?

Aaron broke the silence. 'Sergeant, I cannot confirm that everyone has received emails, but I have.'

A transitory smile came over the Sergeant's face, 'I do not need confessions as I know you all received emails from a site in the United States, which is likely to have been set up by Evelyn Chumley.

Through our investigations with our colleagues in America, we expect to confirm that she set up these emails before her accident.' The room fell quiet. No one moved or spoke. All eyes were downcast as though each person wrestled with their thoughts.

The Sergeant skimmed the faces of those around the table. Aaron straightened his back. 'Have you read those emails?'

'Yes, Mr Matthews, the police know the contents of all of them.'

Candice jerked her head up. 'You're bluffing. If Evelyn set them up, it was before her injury, so she couldn't have expected her accident or the subsequent police involvement. As they arrived less than an hour ago, the police could not have possibly read the contents.'

The Sergeant's eyes moved away from Candice and focused on Dan.

Nervousness gripped him. He closed his eyes and summoned a deep breath, holding it in. What would they say when he revealed the truth? Would they understand it was imperative and that it was the right course of action? From his point of view, there had been no alternative. Forcing his eyes open, he stared at the Sergeant and grimaced, 'I decided. No more hiding what has happened. I decrypted the emails and copied them from the server to the police.'

Ahmed flew out of his chair and lunged towards Dan. 'You damned fool!' He leaned across the table and raised his fist.

Dan glared at him with contempt and pushed him hard in the chest. Ahmed sprawled back in his chair. A heavy hand from a police officer restrained any further movement. Two more officers entered the room.

Dan noted their presence with a weary sigh. Had he made the right decision? Only time would tell.

55

The Sergeant nodded to her fellow officers, who spread throughout the room. 'You will be taken to the police station where you will be cautioned and questioned.'

She waited for the noise to subside as the occupants of the table moved in their seats. Sadie Joiner cried, but the Sergeant showed no sympathy as she had lied previously. 'I have the evidence of the movement and location of the Ziani during Sunday afternoon. We have recently found witnesses who have confirmed that Evelyn was fit and well on her journey back from Scarborough. The car stopped to charge at the Manor near to your former offices. That location is the focus of our investigation.'

She circled the room, staring at each, 'You will be asked about your exact location for that Sunday afternoon. We have evidence about some of your movements, so I advise you to tell the truth.'

Ahmed growled at her, 'Bullying by the police. I've read about it in the newspapers and now I come across it as a personal experience. You are guessing and desperate. When I explain to my Queen's Counsel you will lose your job as the claim against the police will be high.' He rested back in his chair.

Candice snarled, 'Shut up, you pathetic man. I shudder to think what your email from Evelyn disclosed about you.'

The slightest of grins crossed the Sergeant's face.

Aaron thumped his fist on the table. 'Candice, keep your words to yourself. This is a delicate situation and we need no accusations.'

Ahmed waved his pointed finger around the group, 'No one else say a word. If you implicate me in any way I shall sue for defamation of character.'

The corners of Simon's mouth kicked up into a sneer. 'If I were certain that it was you, then I would willingly tell the police, you pathetic man.'

The Sergeant's voice rose above the movement and shuffling, 'You will be taken in separate cars to the police station where you will be asked questions about your whereabouts leading up to the murder of Evelyn Chumley.'

56

Dan rose slowly to his feet, 'Sergeant.'

'Yes.'

'I wish this terrifying episode to be concluded as quickly as possible.'

'You may be assured that the police wish for speedy results. You may give us any further information at your interview.'

All eyes focused on him. He stretched his shoulders. A wave of apprehension swept through him and the anguished faces stretched tighter. It was crunch time and there was no turning back. Sweat beaded on his forehead and he swallowed hard. 'After the emails arrived,' his husky voice became almost inaudible, 'Everyone here read theirs, then I sent them to you.'

The Sergeant nodded and stared at him, her gaze alarmingly direct. Silence filled the room. Everyone waited. The blood drained from Dan's face. He struggled for breath. An imaginary hand had closed around his throat. He forced himself to speak. 'For everyone, a second email also arrived.' A gasp of horror echoed around the room.

Ahmed grabbed at his laptop, but the officer nearest to him snatched it away.

The Sergeant raised her eyebrows in a questioning manner, 'Have you passed them on or destroyed them?' Her voice was low pitched and cold.

'Sergeant, I contacted you to give you as much information as possible and have forwarded them to you, but the contents were the same for everyone.'

Dan gulped, trying to swallow the rising uneasiness that overwhelmed him. 'However, it will take you a great deal of time to find the information without my help. If it's acceptable to you, I would rather elaborate with everyone present.'

'Explain before I can give my agreement.

He struggled to take a deep breath. 'In the second email from Evelyn, sent to everyone, there is a web link to a repository of information that Evelyn had put together. She had created a smaller repository on the server which I found. It contained notes and details about all the people around the table. There was no devastating information only that which could be gleaned by legal means. Not knowing whether it would ever become significant I copied it to my Cloud space before deleting the office version. I inform you of this because she used a sophisticated front end to encrypt and scramble the information. It took me weeks to work my way through her method to reveal the contents. The remote repository uses the same hiding mechanisms.'

Aaron raised the flat of his hand. 'Don't say anymore please, Dan.' His voice loud and unnaturally shrill.

Candice pointed at her husband. 'I agree with Aaron.'

'And me,' added Ahmed.

Sadie gulped and tears glistened on her pale cheeks. 'Please go ahead tell the police everything.' She stared at Dan. 'It will be painful, but perhaps it can draw this nightmare to an end.'

'Why will it take time?' The Sergeant's face didn't reassure him.

Dan pursed his lips. 'It is vast and has been labelled by Evelyn with her strange and elaborate file naming system. As I've had to remove many of her files from our systems, I'm the only one who understands the code she uses. May I show you?' The Sergeant nodded.

Dan slumped into his chair and slid the keyboard on the table towards him. With a trembling hand, he flicked the mouse at the side and the projector lit up at the end of the room. All eyes focused. He pulled up the email and clicked on the link to go to the repository.

He set the mouse to automatically scroll through the list of files. Thousands of files, with non-sensical names streamed from the bottom to the top. 'Carry on, Mr Harding. Do you know the relevant ones to the murder enquiry?'

Dan searched the list and held the mouse pointer over one folder. 'As many in this room are already aware, Evelyn tracked our cars.'

Ahmed shouted with a quiver in his voice, 'I didn't, that's illegal.'

'Shut up, Ahmed,' hissed Candice.

Dan waited for silence to fall, 'But none of us knew that Evelyn also tracked our phones.'

Simon put his head in his hands and stared at the table.

Candice gaped in open mouthed horror.

Dan pressed the button on the mouse. 'Evelyn became an evil genius.' The screen lit with a map of Sheffield and South Yorkshire.

Dan dropped a screen menu and pressed, 'All cars.'

'This is two o'clock in the afternoon that she was attacked.'

The Sergeant's eyes opened wide. 'The file name gives the date.'

'Only because I have decrypted it. I built an app that will decrypt the names so I can search them.' He opened another window. 'That is a list of files on the repository, it will take you months to search through them as there are tens of thousands.'

'Please continue.'

Everyone returned their focus to the map on the screen, 'All our cars are in Sheffield except Aaron's Ziani, driven by Evelyn, which is coming towards the town.' He dropped the second menu and clicked on 'All Phones.' Labelled icons appeared.

Wide eyes stared at the screen in a stupefied silence as the location of their phones was highlighted on the map.

The Sergeant pointed, 'Evelyn's phone is confirmed in Aaron's Ziani.'

Simon's head jerked up from the desk. 'Oh my God.'

They were transfixed by seeing their phones and cars on the map.

Ahmed shouted, 'This would never be allowed in a court for evidence. It's unproven.'

'Be quiet, Mr Khan, or I shall remove you from the room. Carry on, Mr Harding.'

Dan nodded. His throat constricted, making it difficult

to speak, but it was essential to continue. The truth needed to be unveiled. 'The slider at the top of the screen allows me to move it on by ten-minute intervals, which will identify our whereabouts for the afternoon and the position of our cars.'

Sadie whimpered and cried miserably, her face twisted with anguish.

A low moan escaped from Candice's lips, 'No! No more, Dan. What are you trying to do to us?'

'It's over, Candice.' His expression stilled and tension stretched, his voice high and tight. 'We need the truth.'

Horror crossed Aaron's face as a policeman filmed the screen with his phone. Even if Evelyn's repository was destroyed, they would have the film as evidence. Aaron attempted to stand, but the heavy hand of a uniformed officer came firmly down on his shoulder and forced him back into his seat.

Dan's muscles stiffened and his chest rose and fell with rapid breaths, 'Sorry, everyone, but it's time for the truth. I have not watched this before so do not know what happens. ' He continued to click the mouse across the menu revealing everyone's whereabouts at ten minute intervals. The tension in the room increased. No one spoke. All eyes were fixed on the screen.

57

The Sergeant snapped, 'Stop at four o'clock.' No one moved or uttered a single word. 'You each know where you were, but I presume the silence means you are checking where everyone else is.' The Sergeant studied the screen. 'A perfect reconstruction. Unconventional, but I believe that Evelyn will reveal the identity of her murderer.' She closed her mouth and listened to those in the room, waiting for that one indiscretion that could solve her case.

'My God!' Aaron stared through narrowed eyes at his wife. He fixed his astonished gaze on Dan, 'You and Candice were together, I don't believe it.'

All eyes returned to the screen. Sadie's sorrowful voice muttered, 'Sorry, Dan, I'm truly sorry.'

The implication of the evidence was hitting home. The Sergeant received nods from her colleagues that everyone in the room was being closely observed. All faces were wide eyed and pale noting the proof of their whereabouts that Sunday afternoon.

The Sergeant's voice cut across the silence, 'I'm sure you didn't realise you were so close together. Hold it there, Mr Harding. Let me sum up so far.' Her grave frown deepened to a scowl as she stared at each of them in turn. 'We have Mr Dan Harding in his car with Mrs Candice Matthew's phone on the industrial estate at the end of a cul-de-sac that is only a quarter of a mile from the Ziani charger.'

Aaron's loud voice dominated the room forcing all to look at him, 'Our old office was still in our possession, so Sadie was helping me clear it out.'

A grin passed over the Sergeant's face, 'The location of the phones seems precise. They are next to each other and if I remember correctly, they are in the shower room of your former office.'

Candice gave an involuntary gasp and Sadie sobbed.

The Sergeant let the silence return, 'Evelyn is with the Ziani at the charger. There are two cars parked in the hotel car park with a phone in each. It appears Mr Ahmed Khan and Mr Simon Jones were alone. Would either of you like to provide the name of a witness who accompanied you.'

Simon shook his head. Ahmed remained impassive. The Sergeant took a deep breath and let it exhale slowly, 'At four o'clock the car started charging and finished at twenty past. Mr Harding, please continue.'

Dan moved the slider on twenty minutes.

The Sergeant moved to point at the screen, 'Mr Dan Harding and Mrs Candice Matthews are leaving. Miss Sadie Joiner is also moving. Perhaps you would like to confirm you had your phone with you when you crossed the road to near the charging point.'

Sadie sobbed and stuttered, 'Yes.'

Aaron banged his hand on the desk, 'I was about to leave our old building.'

Ignoring his outburst, the Sergeant focused on the map. 'Judging by the positions of the phones and cars, Mr Simon Jones was no longer in his car but approaching the charger.'

She studied Ahmed, 'According to the map your phone remained in your car but of course that doesn't mean that you were there.'

'Are you accusing me of attacking her? I'll have your job for this.'

The Sergeant screwed up her eyes and her lips became taught, 'I'm accusing no one. Your threats to my job are superfluous as my record shows I pursue the truth. I am pointing out you were in the vicinity and had the opportunity. And from the emails this morning you also had the motive.

A tense silence descended on the room.

'Move on ten minutes please, Mr Harding.'

Dan did as he was requested and pointed towards the screen, 'The scale is getting wider as the cars disperse.'

The Sergeant nodded keeping her eyes fixed on the map. 'We believe that Evelyn was attacked at the end of the charge. The murderer disconnected the charge, put her in the driver's seat with her hands draped through the steering wheel. The navigation system was then set to send the car home, which is the house belonging to Mr and Mrs Matthews. Evelyn didn't drive. The car took her bloodied body and parked itself in the garage.'

Aaron raked his fingers through his hair, 'Are we going to the police station.'

'Yes, we are. Thank you, Mr Harding. As you say it will greatly speed up our enquiry. Could you tell me are the other recordings before this time?'

'Sergeant, the recordings are continuous and are still running. As Evelyn is no longer with us there is no one to turn them off so they will only stop when they run out of space.'

Aaron scrunched his face up with evident uneasiness, 'Sergeant. Can we move on with this please? When we get to the police station, I shall wish to call a solicitor to represent myself and my wife.'

'You will have adequate time to summon the legal assistance you need.' Aaron stood up. Ahmed leapt to his feet.

Dan flicked through several screens on his computer, his shoulders hunched, and he frowned, 'Sergeant. You have just revealed that you believe the attack on Evelyn took place at the end of charging. There is another file you may wish to see. I have not looked at the series of them so I have no knowledge of the contents only the labels and file naming convention which indicates it might be relevant.'

'What is likely to be in the file?'

'Evelyn had been extremely clever in snooping on us. She placed surveillance devices in our cars to track us.'

'I realise, Mr Harding.'

'What you might not realise is that for the two Zianis, she captured and transmitted the dashcams and voice recordings from the car.'

'Tell me more as we found no disk in the dashcam.'

Dan nodded, 'The disc would only need to be there for the transmission.' He pressed the file and the screen filled with a picture of the road in front of the charger.

Dan pointed. 'This is the dashcam file for that afternoon

at 1600.'

Evelyn stepped across the front of the Ziani. Everyone gasped at seeing her on the screen. Dan gulped, 'I guess she is moving to plug in the cable for charging. Shall I move the timer to 1620.'

The Sergeant nodded.

The stunned silence was suddenly broken by a chair being pushed over as Aaron attempted to run to the door. He crashed through the first policeman, but two others overpowered him. He struggled in their firm grasp and shouted, 'It's not true.'

The picture on the screen filled with Aaron walking towards the car at the charger.'

Evelyn's recorded voice filled the room, 'Hello, Aaron have you come to pick up the car? Your app would have told you I was here. Did you like my integration?' She appeared on the picture and kissed him on the lips. He frowned at her and led her to the side of the car away from the sight of the camera. Then came only the sound, 'No! No! Aaron please.' Then a muted scream.

THE END

Enjoy this book?

Thank you for reading my book. If you have time I would appreciate a rating or review. They are a great help to me in developing and writing my books.

You can find more information about my books on my website:

T M Goble's Website

www.tmgoble.com

Action Thrillers

Detective Murder Mysteries

Standalone Murder Mysteries

Historical Fiction
Contemporary Fiction
History of Peak District Literature
Seasonal Recipes
I occasionally send newsletters with details on new releases, special offers and other bits of news relating to my books.

Printed in Great Britain
by Amazon

47015915R00118